SEVEN
Diary of an Obsession

SEVEN
Diary of an Obsession

Eliande Jacques

CANISTRIGGER
PUBLISHING

All copies of the book are produced as print on demand by Lightning Source, Inc.

Grateful acknowledgement is given to © Éditions Gallimard for permission to reproduce in Chapter 14 the poem *Cet amour* by Jacques Prèvert, from the collection *Paroles*.

Visit us on the web at www.canistriggerpublishing.com

ISBN 978-91-978707-0-2

Front cover image by Zindy S. D. Nielsen
Back cover image by Eliande Jacques

'For Seven'

Contents

There is always some madness in love. But there is also always some reason in madness.
                                    —Friedrich Nietzsche

Show me a sane man and I will cure him for you.
                                    —Carl Gustav Jung

Foreword

A *journal intime* is where some people write down their thoughts, recognising the ever increasing need to record their daily experiences. In the novel *Seven—Diary of an Obsession* it is also a sort of cathartic process, leading to the final realisation of the central character's emotional and mental state. The man responsible for provoking such turmoil is ambiguous and deceptive, but his equally charming childlike disposition is a source of much confusion for the diary keeper. Like in Shakespeare's *Dark Lady Sonnets*, the object of desire is a dark and mysterious figure, with an impenetrable and captivating aura impossible to ignore.

Eliande Jacques's debut novel is an intense journey into the human nature, a soul searching experience, and ultimately a brave attempt to concentrate different narrative styles into a unique form of expression.

Miss Jacques is both painting and sculpting words, alternating between soft brush strokes and carving chisels. The result is an enthralling, partly surreal tale of love and obsession, a dramatic story of two scarred souls longing to find their place and purpose in a tainted world.

Preface

I thought long and hard about how to present my book, and when I eventually came round to writing the introduction, I realised it could be summarised in a fundamental axiom: love is multiform. One aspect of love is obsession, the compulsive preoccupation with a fixed idea–as the clinical definition goes.

I chose to tell the story of a human soul unable to survive when faced with beauty, torment and final resignation, caused by the unattainable green-eyed man who becomes the focal point of an entire existence. The need to escape the grinding reality of our daily life can become overwhelming, and we look for comfort in the realm of imagination.

It is like embarking on a journey: it can last a few moments or a lifetime. Some of us do safely return, but others get lost in an intricate maze of fantasy and self-delusion, never to be seen again.

CHAPTER 1
The Beginning

I have decided not to write anything anymore. Well then, what am I doing right now? I have felt the deception of the writing art my whole life, sadly never quite able to break free from that childhood spell.

I am a child at heart, trapped in a woman's body. And I feel, feel . . . feel some more. There is no necessity to have feelings, and I would rather not have them at all. It would be downright perfect, almost ideal, if we were born without a heart that feels. As the pain never truly subsides (the pain of living that is), I wonder how pleasant it would be to just feel nothing.

I have many demons. They all suck the life out of me, but the latest one is something far more deadly. He has the face of an angel, feminine green eyes concealing a door to a young, torn soul, perpetually searching for its time and place in this messed up world of ours.

His name is . . . . But I will call him Seven, after the sacred number whose mystic pre-eminence embodies the cosmic meaning of completion.

What is different this time? Hard to explain, really, though I will try. All my demons have beautiful faces; they come to haunt me, slipping into my life without a warning, often as if they were a visible presence, unreachable and untouchable, yet so desirable that I cannot resist them. So, I start my chase and believe me, it has taken me to so many secluded corners of the world.

One of them once hounded me so tenaciously, that my

pursuit ended up in Russia. After pestering me for years, it had forced my life to embark on a chaotic odyssey, blatantly encouraged by an obsessed mind that could not avoid being tricked by this demon's different faces. It confused me, played a clever game of cat and mouse, and in the end, I succumbed. My fate had been decided for me before I could even realise it.

Those monsters . . . They always win, you see.

Others have taken me for a wild ride of a different kind, yet I have never managed a single victory against them. Every time, a piece of me dies; every time, a part of my mind is lost forever, forced out of its shell, surgically removed by them.

I cannot have love. I am alone in this life: that is my fate. I am aware the company of my demons might not provide real companionship, but somehow in these unhealthy relationships I have found my *raison d'être*.[1] I could not exist without being drawn to those fiends; in a rather masochistic exercise of power, I never fail to fall victim to their charm and beauty.

At first, I attributed this codependence to my youth, my immaturity, yet now, as I am on the verge of a midlife crisis, I can see that those ghouls are still here and above all, they have the exact same effect on me as they did when I was a teenager. Therefore, age has clearly nothing to do with it.

Seven is a monster. I could give my life for him: seriously. All he has to do is ask. I would give my life even for that request alone, but it will not happen. The demons never reveal themselves in the flesh, carefully ensuring they are unobtainable and out of reach. Their sadistic impulses are a perfect match for my inborn masochism. It could not be any different.

The story of Seven begins one hot afternoon in the month of July. Just an average, solitary, sweaty afternoon in which my mind did not have the strength to wander too far. And suddenly, there he was: on my TV screen! He was a gladiator, fighting for his life in the Roman arena, barely surviving a battle that he was eventually going to lose.

A face in which a pair of luminous green eyes shone like precious stones: I could hardly breathe. I was choking, suffocating on so much breathtaking beauty. No man on earth could ever be so perfect, I thought, and I was right. I wanted to be there to save his life, to take his hand and rescue him from the lions about to tear him apart. *Mon Dieu! Quel spectacle!*[2]

Yes, Seven is French. My very first demon was also a French one; I must have been only six or seven years old when I encountered him. He too had incredibly pretty eyes, and I enjoyed the pleasure of his company for quite a number of years.

Back to Seven, he fought hard and lost that particular fight, but he won me, a sad trophy to take home. Indeed, not properly a trophy, for he does not even know I exist. I am an illusion, perhaps a distant voice in some nightmares of his, but certainly at a safe distance, so he could never be hurt by me.

It started just like this, with a face on my TV screen that captured my attention, and two months later here I am, addicted to this drug, just about to overdose. It is my wish to do so, I sincerely hope this one will kill me. Once I am dead, no more haunted feelings, no more pain. But until that moment, I need my dose, a shot of Seven any time I can get one. I have no inhibitions, no boundaries exist that will ever restrain all the things I am going to say about his body. This is not a tale for the faint of heart, no fairy tale either. On the contrary, it is brutal, perverse, sexual and raunchy. No respectable human being should read it, then end up cringing at the thought that a woman, raised a Catholic, could ever write such profanities in the light of her demonic obsession. Nothing can possibly justify it. I am the lowest of the low, believe you me. I deserve this punishment, but beware of the powerful weapon I will be using in the attempt at saving myself, the specific instrument being my own twisted mind, fighting hard to escape this hurricane unscathed. Do not pretend I did not warn you. If you turn the page, I am here: in your heads, in your dreams. Once you start reading, there is no turning back. How daring are you?

When I saw Seven again, he was not alone: his mother was with him.

I must now spend a few words on this exceptional woman. First of all, you should take note of her goddess-like status. Yes, I am not kidding you: Seven's mother is divine. She exemplifies the ideal woman: respectable, compassionate, morally irreproachable.

She has fair hair, a light complexion and although I have never heard her voice, I bet she also sounds like a divine

3

creature. I choose to call her Marie, though this is not her real name.

Any good mother ought to be considerate and caring, and Marie is no exception; she is discreet and patient, loving and attentive, openhearted and well intentioned. She must be worshipped as a sign of devotion, for it was her doing that brought Seven into this sad world. Also praised, for making certain he was going to be her one and only creation, the ultimate conception.

On an October day (wild guess) in 1985, Marie and her husband, whom I am going to name François, decided to engage in sex. It is possible she initiated the action, maybe because François was tired or simply uninspired; in spite of this, she made sure his mood would change quickly. After all, she was adamant to take advantage of what in her heart was the right moment to make love to her husband, and as a consequence conceive a child right there, in their beautiful home with a swimming pool surrounded by wooden decking and a magnificent natural scenery.

Or perhaps, they were not even at home. They might have been on an exotic holiday, perchance staying at some nice hotel, all the more contemplating the idea of turning their efforts into something or someone really worth while.

Seven was very much a wanted child: he was no accident!

Marie and François desired, almost demanded it of each other. They embraced only the idea of a boy, a sweet precious boy who would carry on the family name with pride, and would eventually realise all their dreams by becoming a star. The fruit of a wild lovemaking, passionate and intense, almost violent. They knew what they wanted, but Marie was also determined to give life to nothing less than a magnificent human masterpiece.

We owe her, our French goddess whose eyes are probably as green as Seven's. On that October afternoon, what took place was truly a miracle. A man's lucky sperm met an egg belonging to a divine being. And this is how the idea of Seven got started. For that is what he was, back then: merely an idea. Nonetheless, a perfect one. Marie was aware of it, not a shadow of a doubt in her mind. She wanted to be a mother and was asking for a son; she felt it in her guts that the wonder of conception was going to take place. No orgasm could have been more pleasurable than hers, as the idea of what was going to happen to her body flashed through her head.

And so, Seven began growing within her pelvic cavity. How wonderful it must have been to have him inside (I envy her for that). Seven kicking. Seven as a foetus in her womb, viewed in a sonogram, all curled up and sucking his thumb. The X and Y chromosomes . . . The many combinations, what determined his eye colour and the shape of his head, his fingers and every single one of his birthmarks. All that and more was happening to Marie, as her figure changed and kept on changing, but never lost its vigour and flexibility. She was ever so beautiful and suave.

Seven's birth happened in June, a hot month of the year, on a Wednesday. 'Wednesday's child is full of woe.' That is true, my friends. Later on, I will be telling you all about Seven's personality, and you will understand why the old saying is so right, in his case.

The family gathered around the bed, to see the offspring of Marie and François. They were in awe. Never on earth had a child this beautiful been born. They could not explain it, but simply gazed at the newborn baby boy sleeping in his mother's arms and felt elated, as though they too were touched by some divine energy.

The day Seven was born, I was nineteen. I did not know it yet, but it was the beginning of the end: my end. My sweet torturer had arrived into the world, and I was going to be his willing victim, twenty-two years later.

When he was two years old, Dad showed Seven *something* that would make a deep impact on his entire future life. The *something* in question defines in unequivocal terms Seven's own identity, whose design was not forced onto him but merely suggested by introducing the toddler to competitive sports. At the tender age of four, he had already chosen a career; by the time he turned nine the whole world became familiar with his talent, and could not help but expatiate on the subject, very often with a pinch of malice as if to lay the foundations for a future volte-face on the boy.

Unaware of the dangers of letting *the world* into his young life, Seven thought it was wonderful to be so special, and dreamt of great victories and numerous trophies, thanking his

5

parents every day for the opportunity given, living the perfect existence so many other children his age would only imagine possible. For Seven, life was idyllic, the right balance between a happy childhood and an increasingly successful career. Little he knew about the price to pay, or even the price he would make me pay, from the moment he appeared into my life. He grew up in a small town immersed in medieval beauty, right in the heart of Aquitaine, the most south-western region of France. The boy and his childhood chums would often play hide-and-seek, disappearing into the warren of alleyways stacked with stone houses until they were tagged or tried to run to home base.

When puberty struck, Seven was cute and gentle, still nothing like the beast he is now. And yet his beauty, so discreet and humble, was undoubtedly beginning to arouse the lively interest of the pubescent girls around him. They already adored him!

However, Seven was about to leave his hometown for good, pursuing his dreams and ensuring he would realise them in the only possible way: by completely devoting himself to the cause. He felt compelled to accept his father's advice and take the plunge in the big city, where so many other hopefuls were in search of glory. Although, it was not glory he longed for, he just wished he could show the world his skills and in doing so, make his parents proud.

There, every one talked about him and hinted at his imminent success like it was a sure thing. They were almost mesmerised by Seven, like they had not been in years for anyone else. And thus, for the very first time in his young life, Seven began to feel the pressure. It felt like a punch in the stomach. His heart started throbbing with anxiety, as he was suddenly gripped by a sense of nausea: he wanted to throw up. It was awful. He panicked and looked for help: where were Mum and Dad?

Marie–sweet Marie–came to his rescue. Mother knows her child better than anybody else. Mother is there to comfort, to hold him tight and tenderly kiss his forehead, while gently caressing his cheeks. She speaks the right words of wisdom and love, the unconditional love so rare to find. Mother gets rid of the nausea, throws it away, locks it outside the door and makes sure no harm will be done to her baby. Mother: what a wonderful word. The embodiment of peace and security, the word that is akin to a neutral land, where all of us can go and feel protected. And for Seven, his mother was and still is that safe retreat. When he runs there to hide, he becomes the newborn baby again, lying in her arms, sleeping soundly, protected and adored, unaccountable.

When the first success came, Seven was already the talk of the town. The world could not stop discussing the new sensation, they were all at his feet: they literally worshipped him!

He had new friends as well as the old ones; he had the girls screaming out his name, wanting to touch him and more. They would follow him everywhere, asking for his autograph (how strange it must have felt, the first time), and I assume he must have lost his virginity to one of his female admirers. Not that Seven wanted to have the girls chasing after him, at that time. In the end, he preferred the company of his male friends who loved soccer and going to rock concerts; they were not too needy and just accepted him for who he was.

François did not want his son to get too distracted either, therefore kept a vigil eye on him, at times even controlling his life. Seven did not mind it, ergo never complained. After all, his parents were the only people he could really trust.

One can assume that Seven had a normal upbringing, also in the heterosexual sense of the word. Very likely, a Catholic upbringing too. But by the time he was twenty-one, his dark side had begun showing, and very soon he was to turn into the demon that is pestering me here and now. Being a Gemini, the conflicting aspects of his character could not be dismissed too easily. He is two people in one, both inseparable yet constantly battling for supremacy. I lust for his dark side, of course. I am not interested in the other one, I am addicted to the beast, no doubt. But even so, Seven cannot be fully understood without having a close look at the bright, happy side of him. Just do not analyse him . . . ever! He hates it with all his heart. They have tried it already and failed miserably, because there is nothing he despises more than people wanting to dissect him, in an attempt at getting to the core of his personality. There is no use in delving deeper into his subconscious conflicts, it would only lead to detrimental consequences. He wants to be left alone, does not welcome you into his mind, and he will be always rejecting any effort to explain the root of his weaknesses. You see, the key to Seven's mind is to accept its complexity and let it come to you instead. We must just wait patiently for that moment to present itself. Eventually, it will.

Still, time is not on my side, I am urged to find another way. Overdosing every day, brings me one step closer to the end; in my case, the situation could not go on for years, it has to be solved quickly, but certainly not painlessly. In fact, whatever the outcome might be, I will be the one left bleeding. And yet I no longer care about that. I need my drug and like any other addict, it does not matter at what costs. Seven may still be young while I almost resemble an old maid, but his demonic stranglehold will not yield. I have no intention of fighting it either.

We both are only children, one blessed with the gift of life, the other cursed by it. Nevertheless, both prisoners of the infernal spiral, but whereas I am a victim of this unspeakable charade, Seven will soon be the executioner. He is already my tormentor, my sadistic king: you would be fooled by his beautiful face. It is fair to say that there are others who have fallen victim to his power, but none is like me. I am the unfortunate one, whose life depends on Seven, his every action affecting my own existence. Seven is more like a deadly poison than runs in my blood, infecting it day after day. No transfusion could save me. I am doomed. But I could not have chosen a better disease to die from, for Seven is and will always be the son of a goddess, and I–a weak woman–cannot help but bow before a being so perfect and divine.

CHAPTER 2
Transformation

About five months before his twenty-second birthday, warning signs foretelling the dangers of Seven's menacing metamorphosis could easily be identified. Urges of a young man, closeness of people devoting themselves to him and wanting to share a bit of his perfection, all of that made him increasingly aware he had some kind of power to exercise on others.

Seven's body reeks of sex, oozing with desire through the perfect skin. He walks and crashes down the mere mortals, wants them to feel the pain of not having him and gives nothing in return, leaving them hungry and thirsty, willing to sacrifice anything just for a touch, a little glimpse of that harmonious, masculine body of his.

He covers it up, does not show it enough, therefore increasing desire, and the forbidden act of self-loathing, that so many of us perform on a daily basis. If one cannot have him, one cannot help but hate oneself for not succeeding.

Seven was also made for sexual pleasures. More than anyone before him, he has what it takes to give and take sexual fulfilment. I should know this quite well, as the mere sight of an inch of his flesh in a photograph sends waves of orgasmic eruption to my skin, in ways that words cannot even begin to describe.

The expectations for the new year were very high. Seven had set some goals for himself and truly believed he could achieve them.

It always happened like that for him; first, there was some careful planning of future events, then a thorough preparation for them and lastly, the reaping of what had been sown. The careful planning had never let Seven down. Until now . . .

A trip to Slovakia proved to be both successful and full of pleasant surprises for him. But the insatiable hunger of his demon dragged him into a seedy tavern, where many witnessed his shameful debauchery. Surrounded by silly whores and intoxicated by the fumes of alcohol, he only satisfied his dark side and its desire to dominate, which is what by now he had learnt to do quite magnificently. Those slutty girls, their naked bodies: it was all beneath him! A cheap whore can never appreciate the man he has become, yet she insists on ignoring our suffering, using it instead as a vulgar business transaction, generating nothing but bitter resentment. It might sound harsh, but these sexually profligate women are mere commodities with a price tag attached to their bodies (and I am being kind).

One can imagine the sheer horror Marie and François felt after they found out about their son's little Slovakian adventure. The disappointment, the shame. How could he? Their baby boy, their angel. He had sunk so low that they did everything in their power to erase every single trace of the unfortunate episode.

It was not their task to elaborate on Seven's dark side. The demon is real, I see him every day, and lust for him every night. But his parents can only see the angel, and when the demon gets mixed up with whores, it is still their angel they see. They do not know where to look. And even if they did, they would not see what I see.

As far as Seven was concerned, there were no contradictions in his actions; he was simply sending out a message to those who had ridiculed him before, saying he could please himself whichever way he liked. Needed no permission to break the rules. His rules were always meant to be broken by him. Others, who thought he was not strong enough, were forced to eat their words; no matter how that happened, Seven could not care less, as long as he made it clear who called the shots and in what terms.

His parents were a different story, of course. He apologised profusely and kept justifying himself to them, although what he really meant to do was jump for joy and scream his happiness right in their face. Inside, he felt powerful and untouchable. Outside, he looked apologetic and embarrassed. The two faces of Seven at their best.

After the commotion caused by the now infamously known as the *Slovakian incident*, Seven quickly moved on to the next target. And the next one. New tasks, new challenges, going hand in hand with a growing awareness of his boundless libido.

Once in America, of all places, something even more shocking and unexpected took place. Seven wanted to avoid flying to America all along, but in the end forced himself to accept the invitation: his sense of loyalty gave him no other choice. Truth be told, he hated being there with all his heart; his mind kept wandering away, while he felt physically trapped, almost suffocating with an insane rage he had to repress fiercely. Not a single soul perceived his uneasiness. Again, he felt his stomach tighten; a wave of nausea gripped him, as his whole body started to shake, and shooting pains spread throughout his upper and lower limbs, leaving him almost breathless. He tried to overcome that oppressive feeling, but it would not go away. Mother was not there, nor was Father. He was all alone. Alone against the world. A familiar situation indeed, yet not a comfortable one.

If experience had taught him anything, it was to face up to every one single-handedly, and without wavering for a moment, shove his defiant ego in their face. But his plan quickly backfired. All of a sudden, they hated him; they were appalled and insulted by his arrogance. The pain he was feeling became tangible, so he vomited everything he had inside. The gastric juice on the floor, his body not responding, rejecting him. Who was there to help? I was not, though I would have loved to be.

Seven's own world was collapsing before his very eyes, an earthquake of gigantic proportions he could not prevent. He asked himself if his life was going to be like this, from then on. And he got terrified by the answer he gave himself. Everything he knew, all of his certainties were crumbling down under the weight of his personal defeat.

When he returned to France, the sentence had been passed. His fate sealed, or so he thought. Why would they not give him another chance? They claimed they had given him too many already, and he had failed them horribly. Though Seven himself knew it was a lie.

'Let the storm pass,' said Dad. 'Let it rest.' But he just wanted to quit. He thought he did not care anymore, so he began to assess other possibilities.

Fool! He is what he is, cannot change that. I would have told him to get into bed with me, and do to me all the things he wanted to do to them. He would not have disappointed me, I am sure.

But instead of me, he had Marie, his goddess/mother, his safe shore, his anchor, the best friend whom he could never doubt. When she told him to lie down and sleep on it, he followed her advice, henceforth allowing the Sandman to sprinkle magic dust into his eyes, that went on dreaming of unimaginable pleasures all night. In no time, he was ready to be back in action.

A new person entered Seven's world, a few weeks later. In an attempt to revive his interest in the sport, he accepted the kind help of a Monsieur Gilles, a spectacular looking man whose job was to make him hungry for victories again. Seven believed he needed someone younger than his previous mentor, someone more in touch with his world, willing to guide him through the wilderness of future events, which in his mind appeared to be at a great distance, but that in fact were a lot closer than he would imagine. In other words, Monsieur Gilles was meant to be like an older, wiser brother, a point of contact between his will to prove his detractors wrong, and his still quite needy young conscience.

The first big test of the new partnership came shortly after. But again, Seven had to face the firing squad on his own; it seemed his body had given up on him, leaving behind a trail of sorrow he was becoming way too familiar with. *Damn, I cannot do it*, he thought. *I am sick and no one believes me!*

He was right: they did not believe him. They all thought he had found new excuses not to perform; they saw him as an impostor, while he was genuinely hurt. The nausea was there, but he could control it better; he did not puke his guts out this time, just withdrew for a short yet intense moment into the dark area, spitting fire like a dragon, ruthlessly killing everything in sight. Before the firing squad, he embraced the conviction that it did not matter what they thought: all that mattered to him was himself, his parents and Monsieur Gilles.

No, Seven did not flinch this time. He was beginning to learn a new lesson and was loving every minute of it!

Off they went to Rome. So many distractions, the demon fighting hard to be unleashed, and for sure making almost impossible for anyone to restrain him. But in his mind, all that Seven cared about was to finally prove to *the world* that alongside Monsieur Gilles there was a new man, a somehow better and improved version of himself. For a while, we all believed it too . . .

The days went on fine, he felt good, inspired and energetic. Until the gladiator fight in the big arena, which was also the first time I ever saw Seven myself. He was doing so well, fighting, winning, surviving: I was so very proud of him!
Then, something went horribly wrong. The crowd turned against him, wanting him dead. They demanded it, shouted it: 'Seven must die!' A thousand thumbs down. There was no escape. *Why? Why do they hate me?* he thought to himself, as he could sense the old, weak Seven creeping up inside of him. Although he was putting up a fight, he knew in his heart he was not going to win. Hopelessly gazing at Monsieur Gilles, trying to collect his strength and find some inspiration. Searching desperately for the loving eyes of Mother and Father, feeling like a little child lost in a big, dark forest: Seven finally succumbed.

He did not know it, but at that very moment he had me hooked on him forever.

Of course, the last thought on his mind were the adoring women worshipping the ground he walked on. Dejected and disillusioned, Seven contemplated the idea of running away for good, then angrily dismissed it. He was not a quitter: oh no, not my Seven! He was a man, no matter what every one else was thinking, he did what he could in a situation as difficult as that one. He had nothing to be ashamed of. He vowed to himself to take a sweet revenge on all those fools. In the very core of him, there was a fire burning, a fire I could already see. Like flames of hell, his reasons became clear, as Seven took shape into my twisted mind, permanently transformed in the demon tormenting me to this very day.

By that time, I was so obsessed with the shape shifting Seven, I just lived for a glimpse of anything about him. When I had the fortune to see him again (along with Marie), he had poisoned most of my blood and spread out like a terminal disease I could not possibly stop. There is no cure for this illness, no therapy can help. The addiction takes over everything else, it destroys all, manipulates it and finally triumphs. There is no way out, as Seven holds the key to hell, teasing me, torturing me in every way possible. His demon is the strongest I have ever encountered. It is terrifying and blasphemous, a pure sinner. I gave myself completely to him, I am possessed and owned by this wonderful, scary creature.

What followed next was a strenuous search for information, accompanied by a constant barrage of questions I kept asking myself (none of which had any answers). The whereabouts of Seven became my main concern, I often wondered where he was and what he was doing: with whom. I have been so unsuccessful and frustrated all my life that quickly he became my only breath of fresh air, the sole creator of my happiness. The demon had taken over completely and I only lived for him, as I still do, to this very moment.

For Seven another trip to the American continent was around the corner. First, it was Canada. He had put behind all the bad memories and started showing a bit of his strength. How jealous I was of all those little whores hanging on his every word, writing about how they had met him, and how sweet he had been to them, and kind. All them bitches, thinking they could get through to him and actually expose his very soul: they knew nothing at all. They were fooling themselves, expecting Seven to be just how they had imagined, the pretty boy from France, with beautiful green eyes and a killer smile.

But nothing about Seven is what it seems. I know it, and he acknowledges it too, but others could never understand it. They irreparably fall for his good looks and charming ways, swooning at his feet, unaware of his demonic self. That is also my strength, something I could use to my own advantage; as a willing victim of my sweet torturer, I get to see inside the darkness imprisoning us both. It is a privilege and a curse, but it puts me in a favourable position.

I spent two memorable wakeful nights, witnessing a roller coaster of emotions. His victories seemed precious and unexpected. Was that my dark prince? A victorious gladiator, finally able to show the world what he was capable of? Of course, it did not last, but it was worth every single sleepless moment and debilitating migraine I had to endure.

Seven also showed pride in himself and his conquests, something I seldom see from him. Did Monsieur Gilles take the credit for this astonishing turning point? Possibly . . . Though I firmly believe that it was I, willing him on, thereafter giving him all my energy. Once he had sucked up the life out of me, he was back to his average proficiency and I was deprived of every ounce of strength: it is highly demanding to be Seven's slave.

By the time he reached the United States, I was exhausted and so was he. His poor performances were a reminder of the inner struggle ongoing perennially in Seven's mind. The malignant spirit takes over and destroys all of his good work, but he always takes it like a man, for a man he is, spreading his masculinity and forcefulness all around.

We are now back to present time, with Seven on holiday and my poor self shattered, lonely and isolated all over again. Those whores probably waiting in line, as he relaxes before beginning a new chapter in his career. In the meanwhile, my persecution continues at the same pace. There is no rest, no holiday for me. My damnation is eternal, the addiction increasing, the lust more morbid and insane than ever. The alien force has taken over me, with a face reminding me there is unspeakable darkness in beauty. I have devoted myself to the murky soul which brings that face to me. In this limbo, I fight for survival accepting my torture with brave recklessness, stretching out my hand to touch Seven's heart, safely hidden under a thick blanket of lies. They protect its vulnerable membrane, while he thickens his shell with cruel deceptions, the master of disguise that he has become: the angel, the demon. The procedure quickly mastered by him, and with the last layer put in place, Seven's transformation is now complete.

CHAPTER 3
Body Parts

I magine the most beautiful human being on earth. Are you able to visualise it? Otherwise, you could picture in your mind a flawless work of art, a masterpiece, a natural wonder, anything that could inspire perfection while making you more aware of your own limitedness. Anything at all. Whatever you may be thinking of, it would never come within an inch of Seven's beauty. There are no words to describe it: it is phenomenal.

Every once in a while, we witness greatness and are enraptured by the natural perfection surrounding us, but he is something unique, that has never manifested itself before. One single masterpiece, unrepeatable and irreproducible. This is Seven!

He was an extremely good looking child, but an average looking teenager, in my opinion. The demon was dormant and of course, he is the prominent cause of Seven's immense beauty. As a newborn baby, his purity made him irresistible; as a child it was his innocence, but his teenage years were more like a transition between the different stages, paving the way for the big change that gave us the most beautiful creature ever to grace the planet.

When I look at his face now, I see details of rare perfection, and I cannot help but wonder how my own eyes could even be allowed contemplating such a flawless canvas, on which Mother Nature herself decided to paint.

His almost feminine green eyes, the eyelashes so long and

curled, the intensity of that look, undressing me of my whole skin and flesh, until I have only a rabble of internal organs left to show: in that very look hides the demon. There and in his perfect smile; teeth geometrically created, Pythagorean teeth, gates to a world that is in his mouth where I madly long to be and stay, perhaps until the end of my mortal days.

His long tongue, which I can only imagine would bring a whole new meaning to the expression French kissing, is a mastered tool of pleasure for Seven. He has always used it in the most creative way. When words come out of his delicious mouth, whether they are spoken in French or even in English, they are never merely words. Oh, yes! Even when his brain is disconnected, Seven gives birth to melodies so refined and pleasant that they could be compared to music of the highest quality, as though they were compositions by Tchaikowsky, Schubert or Ravel . . . Damn, I am going to be daring: it is like listening to Mozart! *The Marriage of Figaro* in his vocal chords, creating joyful and harmonic sounds, lyrical words designed to penetrate in my ears, finally resting there for all eternity. Immortal nouns, pronouns, verbs and adjectives, spoken in solemnity and full of grace, as elegant as a young Nureyev dancing in *Swan Lake*.

I want to own those words, as well as all the sounds and the melodies they create. I would do anything to hear them all just for me. I would rip my heart out to hear my name pronounced by those divine lips, plump and pink, tasting of whatever chemical combination dwells in his saliva. Those lips alone are worth a hundred lashes and more.

In that sculptured oval of his rises up the majestic nose, the tip of which is round and oddly shaped. He seems to be rather fond of such a nose, a body part screaming of importance and respectability; in fact, he is often caught in the very act of touching or scratching it, thus drawing our attention to it and away from the famous green eyes.

The eyebrows are the perfect frame for those eyes, at times almost distracting, but unlike the green pearls, not at all feminine. There is a tiny mole above his right eyebrow, embellishing his incredibly elegant forehead. I would love to pass my fingers on it, softly kissing it the way his mother has probably done countless times before. Then, with every gently stroke, I would finally reach his temples, slowly massaging them with my fingers.

I love his light brown hair, wild and rebellious, savagely embracing his well-proportioned head; I often imagine my hands running through his hair, grabbing it as he thrusts himself up inside me, then pulling it gently (yet firmly), while tasting his long tongue down my throat.

His body was certainly made for pleasure, but he avoids showing it instead of taking pride in displaying such a natural work of art. Come to think of it, it is far better this way. All the little hussies out there might feel tempted to board it, like pirates would do to a ship carrying a precious cargo. No: I cannot allow that!

It seems that Seven also understands it, and consequently keeps his smooth chest covered up with T-shirts, often soaked with sweat, after the fatigue of a day of work. It is even more challenging to imagine what is hidden, and to an alert eye stealing an inch of his translucent skin would not be an impossible task. It does not take long before someone like me, for example, can master the sophisticated art of stealing. The optical system of my eye operates like a camera; it quickly takes a photo and stores it in the memory bank, where this stolen snap will be kept and cherished with all my heart, until the day that I die.

That chest, his posture . . . On that valley of pure ecstasy, we would all love to rest our weary heads. I, for one, would love to spend endless days and nights just listening to his heartbeat. My ear against his chest would count every throb, wishing that if there were a sound I would have to remember before my departure from earth, it would be only this one. His heart that pounds and pumps blood, sending life through his veins while taking it from me. His heart that feels, no matter what the world says, and aches just like mine, but never ceases to be loud and strong, and above all proud. If it is true the demon never redeems himself, it is also fair to say that Seven accepts defeat in the most honourable way, and cleanse himself of any wrongdoing, real or presumed, taking it like a man, in spite of the lewd gossip engaged by his detractors. I dare them to assert their manhood like he does! There is no contest. It takes a truly great man to lose gracefully and Seven is certainly one, for his heart is uncompromising.

Every square inch of his chest is incredibly hot; indeed, it should be licked and kissed on a daily basis, including those delicious hard nipples to nibble, pinch and suck ferociously; I would slowly move to his glorious belly button (which he would call *nombril*), then further down, teasing and arousing him until he groans with need.

His chest is my territory; drawing my fingers down the edge of his pecs and grazing his skin is an all-round activity that inflames my desire for him, as well as exciting every nerve and fibre on both our luscious bodies.

Many things have already been said about Seven's ass. The firm, round buttocks are mountains of pleasure: I could spend interminable hours just admiring them. He also seems to be comfortable with this particular asset of his; in fact he displays it with immense ease, never failing to generate a variety of comments from the horde of little whores who generally dig his scene. But even men have noticed the exquisite refinement and harmony of the aforementioned, and ever so often a dutiful TV cameraman is instructed to indulge on a close up of that glorious butt. A handful of detailed photographs are also circulating on the Internet, mainly taken by Seven's loyal followers, sharing the same admiration for his delicious backside.

He has legs of an athlete, elegant thighs and perfect feet. And his hands . . . His hands can talk! They converse with the air, smoothly designing lines and intersections, grabbing everything within their reach, and gently caressing the autumn breeze while holding the tool of his trade, which is what makes Seven special in an equally assertive and submissive way. He does use this tool with extreme elegance; his strong arms delivering the goods with swashbuckling panache, assuring proper force is used in accomplishing the task his sport requires of him. A pure vision of grace and class, anticipated by his easy gait, so distinctive and unique. I could spot Seven anywhere, even from afar.

I think Seven bites his nails, unquestionably a nasty habit, yet the idea of those fingers going into his divinely shaped mouth and getting wet with his saliva, constitutes a thought powerful enough to turn me into a horny beast. If only those wet fingers were into my mouth . . . I would lick them up and let

19

them explore me inside and out, they would have free access to every orifice in my body, and would be allowed to tear me apart, touching and poking me senseless. The pleasure those fingertips can give is beyond human comprehension.

What is there between his legs, deserves to be especially praised: I am referring to his undoubtedly perfect cock. As sexual pleasure is what Seven is mostly about, it goes without saying that his love tool possesses some indescribable qualities. As obvious as it may seem, one of them would be its size. Keep in mind the demon has to be well endowed, or it would not be possible to classify him as such, and right now, at twenty-two years of age, Seven has flourished into a spectacular lover. Women and men are equally drawn to him, wanting a taste, needing to touch the single piece of flesh capable of giving them absolute pleasure: could anyone blame them? The ultimate fantasy to fulfil would be to be conquered by his grand instrument, but of course, Seven enjoys teasing them, leaving them hanging on in a sadistic game he loves to play, whenever he senses he is being sought after.

For me, things are slightly different. The demon takes me every night, I spread my legs and invite him in, as willing as a river flowing into the sea. Even though it is Seven the one I would love to give myself to, I accept his demon as well: I still have to have something! I am weak, so is my flesh, and being diseased and on the verge of extinction, I cannot escape my torturer. If Seven were ever going to manifest himself in all his beauty and magnificence, I would show him what a real woman is made of, one who would not only be his lifelong slave, but also a giver, a generous sex tycoon, a missionary and a saint. I would know just how to please my Master and he would never be let down nor disappointed. There is no other living being but me he could completely and utterly possess; no one whose sole life purpose would be his satisfaction and happiness. That gifted, beautiful, promiscuous device of his was made to fulfil my prince's manly needs while subduing the slaves. No wonder its spurt of love juice will taste kind of sweet, with just a hint of saltiness: a perfect ending for the perfect man.

And so, Seven's sex becomes legendary, big and hard and hungry, made for absolute domination, ready to impose itself in a willing mouth or just at rest, to be admired like a Roman sculpture in a museum. Seven–a man in every sense of the word–holds this kind of power, and he can have anyone he wants, anyone at all. He is in command, totally free to make his choice; whatever he pleases he does, deciding the terms and the conditions, pulling the strings, making up the rules as he goes along. He is in complete control, that is where his power comes from. The amazing phallic organ imposing the deal: a totem to the ultimate state of erotic ecstasy.

As French is universally considered the language of love, I would like to pay homage to it, and consequently teach you how to properly name the body parts I have just finished describing.

I am going to list them in my own order of preference, following the lines dictated by my desire and picturing the day I will be speaking those words to Seven himself, probably giving rise to much astonishment on his part. Then it will be my task and pleasure to teach him the same expressions in English, should he not be familiar with their translation already. And judging by the amount of words in his personal English vocabulary, I will assess the damage he would have done, over the time spent roaming the world satisfying his own needs, while destroying the hopes of his deprived slaves.

Now, repeat after me!

Les parties du corps (body parts):
les yeux verts 'the green eyes'
le sourire 'the smile'
la bite 'the cock'
le derrière 'the butt'
les fesses 'the buttocks'
les cils longs 'the long eyelashes'
le torse 'the chest'
le nombril 'the navel'
le visage 'the face'
les sourcils 'the eyebrows'
le nez 'the nose'
la bouche 'the mouth'
les lèvres 'the lips'
la langue 'the tongue'

les mains 'the hands'
doigts et bout des doigts 'fingers and fingertips'
les ongles 'the fingernails'
se ronger les ongles 'to bite one's nails' (this is also
known as *onychophagie* in French)
en grain de beauté 'a mole'
les bouts de seins 'the nipples'
les cheveux 'the hair'
les dents 'the teeth'

Naturally, there are other words and expressions that I find extremely exciting in the French language. Moreover, Seven's voice is so enchanting that if he were to pronounce a name in his mother tongue, even just by accident, he would cause a stir of emotions, and very likely kill some innocent bystander. Nevertheless, to be brutalised and sodomised by his words would be considered an honour, and to die after hearing a sound so delightful would simply be a perfect death. Furthermore, there is no way to describe his accent whenever he expresses himself in the English idiom: if that does not kill you, nothing ever will!

The description of Seven's body might have continued relentlessly for quite a number of pages; if I am leaving out other parts, do not think for a moment it is because there is something wrong with them. Quite the contrary.

Michelangelo's sculptures cannot be deconstructed or dissected to the extreme, one has to witness directly the miracle of his artistic accomplishments in order to understand their beauty. If one were to describe them in great details, it still would not have the same effect generated by standing right before these masterpieces, or by simply admiring them in photographs. The overall beauty is what catches the eye, but after the initial shock, one can begin to appreciate the artist and his mastery in creating such invigorating visions. The immediate visual impact is incomparable.

Michelangelo's marble sculpture of Moses is a perfect example of this. A lifelike creation that prompted the artist to struck its right knee with a hammer and pronounce the words 'Now speak!'

And his stately *David* is another one. It took the great Italian artist more than three years to complete it, but that is insignificant compared to the entire natural cycle necessary to make a body as perfect as Seven's.

He is now entering a wonderful stage in his life, one taking him into the next decade fully aware of his sexual power, strength and beauty. No work of art can possibly match this human masterpiece, the result of several hundred years of evolution, infinite combinations and natural selection.

1986 was the Chinese Year of the Tiger, and Seven is indeed a beast, as passionate, courageous and proud as the animal itself. His body is made for love, his mind completely focused on destruction, impelled onward by the pleasures of the senses; he must continue wandering far over the earth, yearning to achieve absolute satisfaction. Until that day, many of us will have the chance to admire and to long for just a glimpse of what he has become. The demon in full action, beautiful and deadly, ferocious and considerate; like the Tiger, a predator, a hunter who will stop at nothing.

I am at the end of my tether, ready to sacrifice myself. I am here to be taken, abused and finally murdered by my fierce dark prince.

Seven . . . My one and only Master.

CHAPTER 4
The Obsession

The stability acquired through the wilful exercise of a daily routine, is severely tested by the absence of Seven and lack of news about him. He is on my mind when I go to sleep, and when I wake up his energy is more enticing and vital than I can imagine, thus pulling me through the day, as the addiction grows into obsession.

I need him more than food, water, air; I have to inject him into my system if I want to be able to function. It is uncanny how very little is still known of Seven's power; a study has to be carried out on how he has developed into his current self, and I am the scholar whose dedication and commitment cannot possibly be questioned.

A considerable number of photographs are in my possession, and though I have never counted them, I reckon they may be getting close to a thousand. They range from the time when he was a child–living with his parents in his charming home town–to the present, also including his adolescence and some family snaps. No matter how swiftly I scroll through those pictures, Seven's transformation throughout the years becomes increasingly obvious. The most recent photographs depict the demon he has changed into, whose eyes conceal the incomparable power making head turns, women faint and men wishing they were him. His beauty so devastating, every single look at that face is a mortal wound to the eye. He is a man on a mission and no matter what his words might say, deep inside he knows perfectly well his happiness depends on the annihilation of every single mortal soul. No one can possibly resist him: no one ever does!

Many slaves are susceptible to his magnetic force and inevitably feel attracted to it; some may even get very close and touch him, sharing a brief moment of elation. There are others (and I am their leader) who will never be able to get so lucky. We are cursed and will be dying of deprivation, our blood irremediably infected, our bodies forcefully weakened.

This drug with green eyes will push me to my demise in no time. I cannot tell how long I have got left, although I suspect I am getting closer to the end each passing day. If there were a devil, a universal dark force so powerful to call upon and ask for a favour, I would submit to it. Without the shadow of a doubt, I would invoke and demand the prowess of the most evil being just for a chance, a single chance to be allowed complete obedience to Seven. To him in the flesh, not his demon, that is.

As I get further into his head, I learn about his ways by studying the personality; I dig my claws into the complexity of his character and sense the destructive nature of my desire, its tendency to burn pieces of my own sanity, quickly reduced to ashes.

What is left of my old self? Perhaps only an obsession so implacable and cruel, forcing me to neglect every other activity, even the most trivial one. I breathe Seven into my lungs and he becomes almost like a cancer, and at the same time, he is the only hope I have to be cured from the disease. I cannot give him up: I need him in order to survive.

I want his soul, his mind, I crave his heart and blood. I need to drink, to eat and inhale him; the smell of his skin is what inebriates the spirit, before I lose myself in his strong embrace. I am getting increasingly tired of his demon pounding into me in a fierce paroxysm. Seven has to hear my plea! I cry out his name at night, ripping my clothes off, pulling my hair, cutting my skin and bleeding, and when the morning comes he is gone, engulfed by the light of day, while my damnation and agony are left intact. No spawn of hell to offer a helping hand, no celestial angel either, just the utter emptiness closing in upon me.

My devotion to Seven is absolute: there is no other man for me. He is my first, the last, the beginning of the end and the end that begins. Back to front, front to back, only he exists. His perfection, so humiliating for the rest of humanity, is mine to praise and celebrate. The whole world became his kingdom on the day he was born, and so it will be until the day he dies. But even after death Seven will remain on this earth; his power, his energy, the memory of his beauty, they will live on beyond the boundary of extinction.

This is the nature of the obsession. And that is where the chronicles of the addiction begin, history unfolding as Seven continues in his quest for total domination, while pursuing the glory in his chosen sport.

My time ends where his begins. The account of current events and their effect on my life—all the more vivid and real—is what you are about to witness. But always keep in mind that Seven maintains many of the qualities of a real person, although in my head he is almost a fictional character, an abstraction turned real, destined for success and worshipped by many. He has been doing all the things he usually does, since the day he became a professional sportsman; in his head, there are thoughts he cannot really explain, sensations he does not want to understand.

Right now, at this very moment, he is having dinner with Monsieur Gilles and the rest of his team. He will eat his food, then retire to his hotel room and lock the door; before falling asleep, he will relax playing some games on his laptop computer, waiting for Morpheus the Sandman to give him only pleasant dreams, keeping nightmares at bay. Then the new day dawns, his routine begins again, the well-established training regime never fails. The only boost he needs to keep up with his busy schedule, is a brief chat on the phone with François and Marie, his adoring parents.

Seven will have a training session tomorrow, laughing and joking with Monsieur Gilles and nothing will faze him. What he does naturally is what I am addicted to; who he is on this earth, is what I am obsessed with.

I will be providing you with a sample of my own personal hell, and at the same time will give you an idea of how much I need this torture. You will not be disappointed. I am going to bare it all . . .

Third week in August:

Seven is in New York. It is where the new quest begins, after his holiday spent playing golf and acquiring a few more slaves. Back to business now, no time to waste partying. The Big Apple awaits: Seven wants to take a bite!

After several weeks of longing for anything concerning my handsome prince, a few interesting photographs have surfaced. They were taken only yesterday, undoubtedly by one of his many drooling whores. Seven was pictured during one of his training sessions, shirtless, sweaty and as desirable as ever. My Seven, who usually keeps his perfect body under wraps, was displaying it proudly on the training ground, and those tarts could not believe their eyes: neither could I!

Ever since our demonic relationship has begun, I sense that he can hear my thoughts and act accordingly. I did say I wished he showed more of his body, I know, but I only meant he did it for my own private, exclusive viewing. Still, he uncovered it and sent out a most disturbing message, one that catapulted my obsession beyond all the boundaries of reason. He also wore that necklace again, a silver chain with a rectangular pendant, embellishing that long neck of his. Simply stunning!

His hair was as wild as ever, and in his eyes the demon was very much alive, so real one could almost see its reflection.

Seven is blossoming into a kind of man the world has never seen before. What will the world think of his perfection? Will it be stunned, confused, terrified, mesmerised? How many willing victims will there be of his irresistible beauty and the trail of destruction it leaves behind? It will be carnage. This man, this *sex on legs* man, who was made for absolute pleasure, is a death sentence, irreversible and final. Why do we always feel bound to all those things meant to destroy us? What kind of pathological masochism is this? I can only answer for myself. I am sick, mentally ill, seriously disturbed, you name it . . . But I seek no help of any kind, I am just embracing the sickness and delaying my final hour. I would rather have been born without a heart, and only my demise would end the anguish caused by having feelings. I am writhing in despair, yet I simply cannot rip my heart out while I am alive.

The excruciating pain of loving Seven, while harbouring his demon and feeling alive only whenever he decides to grant me a slice of life, is worth every aching moment of the agony. All in all, I must pay a price in order to witness so much beauty, and I could not expect to be treated any differently. It is an honour to be possessed by Seven, a privilege for which many slaves would simply die for (as I would too).

What is he dreaming of right now, while lying on his bed? Waiting for a new day to begin, he is preparing for the next journey to glory, as the battle wages on within his own confused mind. The detractors are only waiting around the corner, ready to attack as soon as he fails to win, and I know he is struggling to find the inner peace necessary in order to succeed.

They interviewed him, hinting at his weaknesses yet again, but he strongly rejected the accusations, told them the past was long gone, that all he wanted was to look ahead, pointing at the victories now within his grasp. With Monsieur Gilles by his side the time is ripe to take revenge on those fiends, the ones who have hurt him by questioning his very nature. They do not know Seven is a winner: they are in for a big surprise. My tormentor is ready to unleash an attack on the sceptical world of sore losers who have deemed him unfit to fight. Hitting back with ruthlessness will be awesome.

I long to be a voice in his dreams telling him to prepare for battle; I would be whispering in his ear at night, breathing my love and devotion into his complex, tortured mind fiercely struggling to figure out its many different aspects. All he has to do is call for me and I will be there, to show him the right way to go. We are interlaced now, we need each other; the connection cannot be broken. Seven reigns over me and I, enslaved by his beauty, am offering my life, the most precious gift I have. He only has to say my name, and I will let darkness embrace me forever.

Fourth week in August:

The big showdown for Seven. I have been waiting all day, unable to focus on anything else; I have been imagining him getting ready to enter the battlefield and show the world the new, self-confident, adamant to succeed Seven.

He started marvellously well, fighting back whenever he was down, I definitely saw the fire in his eyes: the demon in full mode. Then, something happened in his head, there came a sudden yet familiar doubt, stirring up turmoil, confusing him to the extent of making him think of failure and defeat, and of all the things his detractors are going to say as a result of that. The hesitation comes usually unannounced, but never misses an appointment. As a result, Seven's hand trembles, his body does not respond to the brain's movement commands, as the nausea grips his stomach. The fire is soon extinguished and what I see is little Seven, the boy, the insecure, uncertain kid so afraid to disappoint. The demon destroys and kills whatever in sight, sometimes it shatters his confidence and the self-belief so important in an athlete's life.

My heart started to cry and nearly choked on its tears; I felt so helpless because I was not there, and because I knew his defeat would mean goodness knows how many more weeks of abstinence, following Seven's absence from the scenes. For any addict going cold turkey is not a pleasant thing.

Seven lost, was wiped out, humiliated yet again. The bitter taste of defeat in his mouth is all he knows, these days. He needs me, my prince: I am the only one who could help. I would speak just the right words to him, hoping to unlock the door to his future greatness. I am his slave, his worshipper, the humble servant, the submissive subject. If he does not allow the demon taking advantage of me, he will never be free. Why can he not hear my voice? I shout as loud as I can, but we are too far apart, so he will never profit from all the good things that I could offer him.

In defeat, I love Seven even more. He turns me on, inflames my desire for him beyond reasonable comprehension. I want him more than ever. He needs me more than his own blood. Without me, he will be lost, but I would find him no matter what. I would search high and low until my Master is ready to return to me.

He must be feeling pretty dejected right now; in no time, the ones who despise him will set new traps for him, and he will inevitably fall into them, like he always does. The usual derision, the unjustified hatred: he will face it all for the umpteenth time. In his still very young life, he has fought against the prejudice of his detractors countless times, therefore he is well aware of what to expect, and has prepared himself for the worse. Yet, in spite of previous knowledge, it will not be pleasant to be pilloried in public: it will hurt. And he will puke his guts out again, no doubt about that either. But his beauty so undeniable and real, will make him stand tall, unbent as he takes the beating. My Seven, the brave, the valiant, will not flinch. So go ahead, and spit all your venom right in his face, you good at nothing people, so envious of his perfection. Nothing you will say could undermine my faith in Seven, my love and adoration for him are a steel suit of armour, that will protect us both from your perverted attacks.

I have just seen him, putting up a brave face, as the interviewer was collecting his thoughts after the defeat. He was answering politely, talking suavely, looking very relaxed; then, as the man was formulating a new question, he glanced at the camera for an instant. I froze the frame at just the right moment, then printed it out. Oh my, oh my: the eyes of the demon, staring right at me! There is no doubt in my mind that this is a message, as clear and unmistakable as death itself. My Master is telling me he feels my love and all is well with him (or at least, with his dark side). Is it not always the case? Poor Seven, he cannot really fight it, can he? And why should he, anyway? It was there, right in front of me, the green pearls shining like they have never done before. *Il est deçu, mon amour.*[1] Yes, perhaps disappointed in himself, but I am not. I saw it in his eyes, the thing I fight against and embrace at the same time. Right there, in the green valley where I long to see my own reflection one day. The grass needs the dirt to grow; my eyes are the soil, his are the young plant. Our love will be the water, our passion the fertiliser. At one with my Master, fulfilling my destiny, giving myself to the only man who can ever have me. I have seen it, felt it, have become a part of it. I no longer exist and if you are looking for me, you will find me in Seven. I am his symbiotic incarnation.

I have now extrapolated three frames from that video interview, and could not help noticing that when he gives the piercing glance, his facial reactions do not seem to visibly change; in the eyes of the demon a burning desire to explode is discernible, a tangible element of restlessness is also detectable. Rather obviously, on the outside Seven is forced to show a certain aplomb, even under such difficult circumstances. He is able to perform the trick in quite some style, actually. It comes naturally to him swapping between one side and the other, he never has to force it, for one can say this is a skill he was in fact born with.

Before it slips my mind, I want to write about something I found immediately indicative of the degree of my obsession with Seven. I know for a fact that he enjoys listening to music, especially before getting involved in his various activities.

Yesterday, as I was waiting to see him, I was zapping through some music channels, and out of the blue there was a video of a song by a relatively famous British band. Since his passion for this particular rock group is common knowledge, I considered it to be a good omen (although it clearly was not, as his day eventually ended up in disaster). The funny thing is that today I came across another song by the same band, and here is the remarkable thing: the green eyes are mentioned in it! Of all the songs in the world, I had to listen to this one: it makes my hair stand on end. Such an important sign is meant to conjure up a dark force inviting me to spring into action; I cannot ignore the strength of my subconscious mind power, it would be criminal to ignore the subliminal message in this piece of music.

The song dates back to 2002, when Seven was only sixteen years old, hence completely unaware of the kind of man he was soon going to become. I am convinced it was not a mere coincidence to accidentally listen to this particular band, and even if this was just a random occurrence, it shows how the connection between us is strong, despite my unfortunate circumstances (and by that I mean my codependency and addiction).

Seven will wave goodbye to the Big Apple. I have heard he is flying to Japan first, then to China and finally Singapore. So many more miles between us, so many more days hanging on a tiny thread, hoping to see his face, hear his voice, as the demon will possess me over and over again, leaving me breathless and sore.

How am I going to live through each day? I do not really know, as this is uncharted territory for me, I have never experienced anything of this kind. All the previous demons would every now and then relax their hold, but this one will not let go. Seven has got an immense power, a might that he has no intention to voluntarily relinquish; he is determined to destroy me and everything else getting in his way. He is merciless, that much I know and am sure of.

My only hope is to die before he kills me, and that is a whole new chapter, possibly even a whole new book to write.

The obsession never gives a moment's respite, it never stops. This sickness has roots, too deep and strong to be eradicated, and I, this weak and needy woman, have no intention to dig into them. All I want to do is love my Master, hoping with every new day that comes and goes, a little bit of me gets closer to him, until the moment he will no longer be a shadow but the man I have been waiting to die for, should he ask me to, while melting his green eyes into mine. Only then my obsession will end and freedom will be a luminous smile, rested on the lips of an angel, tasting like his sweet kiss in the warm summer rain.

CHAPTER 5
The Real Seven

Exactly three years ago, having barely turned nineteen, Seven moved to Monte-Carlo. He bought himself a luxurious villa with a view of the French Riviera coastline, ideally located in a secure, quiet community, not too far from his favourite golf course. Rather quickly he concluded that the tranquillity and seclusion of the place were just what he needed in his life (not to mention the advantage of not having a greedy tax man at his heels).

His parents must have definitely helped him to settle into life in the exclusive neighbourhoods; he was taking an important step into adulthood, and they would not have missed it for anything in the world. These days, his *pretty den* in the Principality of Monaco has become the ideal place to relax in style and unwind, while playing golf with his chums.

Seven has got quite a refined taste for beautiful things: beauty matters a lot to him. He also loves a comfortable life, an active one, nonetheless, so every minute of his day is spent engaged in some kind of activity. There is never a dull moment for him.

Since the day he was born, my Master has been fulfilling a destiny laid out for him by the stars in heaven. Magic and divination have a lot to do with it, and as matters stand, it has no relevance whether he believes in the astrological gibberish or not. Bear in mind that from the very moment he came into this world, nothing has ever been accidental or unplanned; the position of the planets at the exact time of his birth and their ongoing influence have combined to cause the changes in his personal history, hence leading us to the current state of affairs. Thus everything had been predisposed for the arrival of this perfect creature, and purposely so.

On that glorious day in June and right at that hour of the morning, the Sun was in the eleventh House (prelude to a successful career) and the Moon in the ninth (the peace and quiet of the family life, the love of his mother). It all made perfect sense, and obviously I had a complete picture of the situation way before I found out all the details about it, for I have always been able to read my Seven like an open book. His Ascendant in Leo explains his sexual hunger and it is uncanny that his Chinese sign is also represented by a feline: the mighty Tiger. Seven's given name means *brave* and *powerful*, characteristics also naturally associated to the Big Cats.

And then there is the number 7. In numerology, his full birth name converted into a number will give 7 as a result, and that cannot be an accident either. It seems that both Marie and François knew what they were doing, when they named their baby boy. His life path number (the result of adding the day, month and year of his birth, then reducing the number to a single digit) is 3. It makes him a resilient, strong-willed man, able to bounce back from the setbacks occurring in life and ready to start again with new-found enthusiasm and energy. It is so very true of Seven.

But what is it that makes him so perfect and unique? And why does he have this devastating effect on other people? I wish I knew exactly how to describe this extraordinary young man, but the picture is still confused and knowledge of the real Seven still too scattered.

He certainly loves his mother; she is his rock, the one person who can understand him without words. They have no intention to cut the apron strings, therefore their bond of affection will never be severed, no matter what life will have in store for them. Marie is a goddess, a protective mother and a conscientious caring woman; she knows aspects of Seven's personality that will never be revealed to any of us worshippers. She has access to details of his intimate life and owns all the photographs, newspaper clippings and little objects that have paved her son's life path thus far. Facts and memories she will never share with anyone, secrets only she knows; this woman, this materfamilias, magnificent maker of Seven who we look up to and adore, she is his point of reference, the North Star, the right way to follow.

On the other hand François, his father, is a figure shrouded in mystery. One thing is certain though: his influence on Seven has been enormous. He has always been a controlling man, proud of his son but also quite keen on planning his life for him, despite the inability to fully understand his incredibly gifted boy. Seething with rebellion, Seven's heart was learning to find its own way out of innocence into the threshold of the world of desire. His father had taught him the facts of life, but treated him like a child even when a child he was no more. Maybe he just wished (on a more or less unconscious level) to prolong the childhood, expecting–like most parents do with their kids–his son would always need his guidance and structure. But Seven has got an independent mind, fully self-sufficient, and although he can act like a child whenever he wants to, he is a man aware of his own power and capable of using it in the most destructive way. He has mastered the art of manipulation and turns to it at will. Even his own father can be fooled by Seven's unbridled treacherous side.

François is fifty-seven years old (only sixteen years older than I am), and the best thing about him is that he is still married to Marie, loving her every minute of the day, ever since the first instant he laid his eyes on her and she reciprocated the look. It was an unforgettable moment, relived almost daily in the film of his memory.

He can never forget the heart-warming feeling of holding Seven in his arms for the first time, his baby boy with green eyes who looked at him with nearly a smile on his pretty, little face. François was in seventh heaven, never a joy so intense had inebriated his heart. To this day, his heart melts every time he gazes upon his son's beautiful face, as he convinces himself over and over again that this creature has been the result of his own doing. Of course, he could not be more wrong. Seven is not his property: he has never really been. He does not belong to his father, and François cannot understand this, because it is a concept too difficult to grasp for a man who sees in his son the continuation of the progeny.

As Seven was growing up, his father's influence on him exceeded all limits, thus persuading François the boy would always need his advice and direction. Little he knew about Seven's increasing power over other human beings, not to mention his desire to use every means possible to conquer any poor soul who would fall for his unique and lethal beauty. Occasionally, the old man appeared to be rather self-conceited yet somewhat naïve, as he spoke in place of his son, causing unnecessary embarrassment and trouble. My Master himself had to rescue his father from further humiliation: quite an ironic predicament, if I do say so myself. My handsome prince never really needed anyone; he just pretended he did, to please his beloved father who lived under the illusion of being his maker. We all agree that he could not have been further away from the actual truth.

Seven must have been around eleven or twelve when he discovered what in French is called *l'univers de la masturbation*: the universe of masturbation. Like any other normal boy, he had a fascination with his own body and felt the urges and needs so natural to all of earth's living species. His body was changing fast, the demon becoming stronger: his hunger insatiable.

Through teenage years the exploration of his body was a time for excitement and discovery; the results of the self-love practice became highly rewarding for Seven. He always found a quiet place where undisturbed, he would enjoy all the sensations his body was experiencing before, during and after masturbation; he would use his vigorous hand to stroke his own love muscle as his breathing shifted to more shallow and quick. Soon, he learnt all the different strokes and how to reach an orgasm that left him panting but oh-so-happy and fulfilled. His masturbatory techniques–like everything else in Seven's life–improved and progressed constantly.

The duality that makes him so unpredictable also developed further during those years. His defensive mechanism became quite clear too. On the one hand, Seven appears to deal with defeat with nonchalance, almost resulting careless and superficial, but on the other hand, an endless war is being fought inside of him, and that struggle often turns into a sickness, one that carries also some physically debilitating side effects. His body lets him down and all the things he deftly managed before, he suddenly cannot deal with any longer. The public opinion, his detractors, even his own family: they all make him feel sick. He cannot lose control of his life, will not hand it over to anyone, because Seven exists for one reason, and this is all he will be granting us. His reason and our purpose fit perfectly. We live for him, he works and fights to lift our spirit: this is the game that we play, my friends. And he recognises the extent of his power; he has weighed and counterchecked it numerous times, thriftily making the best he could of his gift. No one can rob him of what he has accomplished so far, but there are traps (so many of them) which will have to be carefully avoided, and perhaps they are the only real danger lurking in the shadows, in that competitive world of his.

The real Seven is a combination of elements making him attractive and intriguing, although on the surface he would be nothing of the kind. For some, he is just one of the guys, but for others he stands above the rest. When he was a young boy, there were many expectations; there still are now, but they keep on changing as often as the changes he goes through himself. However, there might be some people who have stopped believing in him altogether, and who are firmly convinced that the promises of the young age were just an illusion.

He always felt an earnest desire to please every one, searching for any available way to keep his dear ones happy, but only after his recent coming of age he has come to realise how unrealistic it was to waste so much time on such a daunting, Herculean job. All he really can do is satisfy himself, strive for that fulfilment and ignore the rest. The rebellion stirring inside pushes him to break free and become a man, but the demon provides plenty of distractions leading him astray, regardless of the consequences. It is time for Seven to stand his ground, he must vent his rage to free himself from the anger once and for all. He cannot waste his life in the vain attempt to make others happy: our happiness comes from the mere fact that he exists. We are thankful for that and it is enough (although I am demanding more, being the one infected with the disease, therefore not as reliable as the other slaves).

He must embrace his fate, his spirit must rise above dejection and continue the march on the path to glory. I only wish I could lend my support and give him the extra push he needs. I am his counterpart; after all, I have been there too.

It is not easy being an only child; some of us cannot stand the pressure and need to build some protective walls around ourselves. Others deal with it directly, and in doing so they alienate their loved ones. Parents place a great deal of responsibility onto the one child who is supposed to become everything they could not. There is no one else to share the burden with, only us, alone and with no others to relate to. We learn to cope with loneliness, create our own imaginary friends and hope to acquire the skills that make us face up to the lonely years ahead, when the only reference we have ever had will no longer be there. We want to please our parents and ourselves, something that could never be done. It is a lost fight and we know it, we are just too afraid to admit it.

It is fairly easy to imagine the excitement of a family longing for a child who will finally come and turn the darkness into light. And on top of that, just to make things considerably more complicated, he also proves to be the most beautiful creature in the whole world. That child has his work cut out for him.

Seven never yielded to the force of the irksome task, but he also had to learn about the lost child before him, whose ghost would be haunting him for many years to come. It is the sad tale of a lovely creature, destined to never see the light, some kind of ethereal being that had to give way to Seven, because this was its fate. Do you now realise how precious my prince is to his devoted parents? How could they ever let him go when there is no other like him?

The passion in his blood is only destined to explode into a hurricane of physical energy reaching the highest point, and torturing more destitute souls that we could have ever predicted. By the time of his twenty-third birthday next year, Seven will have peaked both in beauty and talent, he will have already reached a pivotal milestone and travelled extensively throughout the globe. Intuition and logic make such prediction possible, though nothing could prevent despair from taking firm hold of the poor souls I share the same torment with. We have been chosen to witness this monster's ultimate victory; we have a mutual interest, a desire to inhabit a world encompassing Seven's glory and might. 'Thy fate is the common fate of all; | Into each life some rain must fall.'[1] When events begin to unfold, I will nod my head and think how right I was to have chosen him as my fearless torturer. I have predicted every step of his way to complete domination, including the ones he will take to tread on me one last time; my own personal angel of death could not have been more real and yet more far away, in the loneliness of my despair which increases every hour, thus reducing life to a desolate make-believe. This fathomless deception has enslaved me indefinitely, still Seven's stopwatch has begun its countdown. Will I be granted a stay of execution?

When he was a child, it must have been amazing to have him around, watching him grow and turn into this talented young man, whose intriguing ability to bewitch became a recognisable personality trait that cannot be disregarded. His versatile nature has never changed, making him not much different from the child that he was then. One day, not too far away now, he will emerge from the cocoon a brand new man, resolute, assertive, invincible. How I wish to be there when it happens . . .

Until that day, the fragility of his mind will inevitably be leading him into this topsy-turvy path, made of continuous highs and lows. And yet, he is forced to stay true to himself; he can only be honest while fighting to keep his determination to succeed. It is hard, I know, when faced with so many contradictions, so many doubts; harder than anything, as he also must keep up appearances, pretending more often than not, to be absolutely fine when instead right there, into his stomach, tongues of fire keep his desire to explode at bay. So he bites his nails and scratches his head, pronouncing words that have been memorised to be spoken only out of convenience: he is the best deceiver I have ever encountered, bar none.

There is no better liar than him in the world, but if you are lucky enough to be shown his other side, you will also come across the most genuine, sincere, utterly dignified human being you could envisage. Remember: Seven (even the mundane one) is a human dichotomy. And this is the very reason why his road will never be straight, for there will be turbulence in a clear sky and rogue waves in his ocean, making his journey a rough one. He will show the scars and bruises from the bumpy ride through life, my proud warrior, my hero. I hope I will be there, beside Marie and François, to witness the miracle that is Seven–the remarkable human specimen–to either celebrate his accomplishments, or wipe away the tears of shame after suffering a stinging defeat. We, the prisoners of love, are players on Seven's stage, eternally trapped, endlessly performing in this comedy (occasionally a tragedy), that has brought us together, unlikely partners yet united in our undying love for the boy with green eyes. The child, the man: our supreme saviour.

CHAPTER 6
The Here and Now

I have established a contact with Monsieur Gilles. I do not know until when the connection will stay open, though the mere fact that it does exist at present time, is definitely a better thing than nothing at all.

Gilles appears to be very kind, even considerate and caring, but ultimately he does not know me nor will he ever be aware of my obsession with Seven (for the time being, this is an absolute certainty). If he ever suspected the level of my insanity, he would be interrupting our contact at once, something any normal human being would be naturally inclined to do. If I am lucky and persistent enough, I might even succeed in creating a direct channel with Seven himself, though this is a remote (nonetheless plausible) possibility. In all likelihood, an outcome so positive and unexpected would jeopardise the completion of this book. Then again: what would you expect? Do you really believe I would care about all of you perverts reading these pages, when I could be with my Master and serve him for the rest of my mortal days? You mean nothing to me. He is my everything. Guess who I would choose . . .

However, let us not get caught up in the entanglements of a purely hypothetical situation.

Ironically, Seven is in Slovakia again, but I assume he will be a lot more careful this time around; mindful of past experience he will not make the same mistake, even though he is the kind of man who tends to relapse into error, unless forced to overcome the need to sin by someone as forceful and devoted as

I would be.

Monsieur Gilles is a faithful and reliable married man. He deeply loves his family (especially his wife), and is devoting an enormous amount of his time to the assistance and help of Seven. This is a mighty, almost impossible job since my torturer does not really wish to be helped, and in the unlikely instance that he did, I would be the only one capable to perform the task. Still, Gilles works for his money, while missing his loved ones immensely. All that for the ungrateful, cruel, perfect man that is my Master. How could he possibly deny him his services? No one can resist the call; to be Seven's slave is the ambition of many and only a few chosen ones manage to turn this dream into reality. After all, it is a logical consequence to neglect all others, no matter how important or meaningful they might be. Seven becomes the only one, the emperor, the supreme king in a world made of beauty, deception and sexual hunger; the irresistible, ravenous wolf forcefully taking its preys, ravishing and devouring them until there is nothing left. He knows no mercy: the face of an angel, the voracity of a primitive beast.

The obsession has been nurtured today. I saw Seven and heard his voice briefly; after spotting the lonesome figure in the crowd, I enjoyed a few minutes of well-deserved, pure ecstasy. Unbelievable! He is getting more handsome each time I see him, nothing can put a stop to that which is his constant ascent to supreme perfection. My mind is insanely lost!

I have degenerated to the point of having an argument with one of those little tarts claiming to be part of his posse of followers. In all truth, she is nothing but an impostor, since she has also revealed to be an ardent devotee of one of Seven's main rivals. How can this be possible? It is a huge contradiction, not to mention an insult to the incomparable perfection of my Master. Anyway, this stupid slut provoked me; I finally was pushed over the limit and lost my patience, so I wisely decided to cut short any communication with her. I realise I could have gone on and crushed her, but it would have taken time away from the real purpose in my life. There is no way I could ever allow that. So perhaps she is now convinced to have won the confrontation, and I will let her remain under this illusion, for I am after something far more grandiose, a reward she could never possibly claim. I have become as ruthless as my handsome prince and have no time to waste on this kind of triviality: I simply pity that foolish girl.

On his battlefield today, Seven was less than impeccable but came through victorious, and that is what matters. One step at the time, right now he cannot rely on his previous planning but has to live each day as a single challenge. He cannot afford to make long-term plans, and neither can I. We are so alike, my torturer and I, to the point whereby we almost melt together.

The feeling of sickness is increasing; just hearing his words, as he conveys his many thoughts into phrases, turns my stomach inside and out. His beauty is so magnificent at this moment. It is almost exaggerated, illegal, utterly sinful. He should be burning in hell for being so beautiful: there is no other way of putting it. I could only wish to live in a constant dream, where Seven's perfection will never wither nor cease to be. How can I even begin to describe it? By enlisting the help of the poet John Keats and his 1818 poem *A Thing of Beauty (Endymion)*, I am hoping to make you all understand what I am talking about. Here is an excerpt from Book I:

> A THING of beauty is a joy for ever:
> Its loveliness increases; it will never
> Pass into nothingness; but still will keep
> A bower quiet for us, and a sleep
> Full of sweet dreams, and health, and quiet breathing.
> Therefore, on every morrow, are we wreathing
> A flowery band to bind us to the earth,
> Spite of despondence, of the inhuman dearth
> Of noble natures, of the gloomy days,
> Of all the unhealthy and o'er-darkened ways
> Made for our searching: yes, in spite of all,
> Some shape of beauty moves away the pall
> From our dark spirits. Such the sun, the moon,
> Trees old, and young, sprouting a shady boon
> For simple sheep; and such are daffodils
> With the green world they live in; and clear rills
> That for themselves a cooling covert make
> 'Gainst the hot season; the mid forest brake,
> Rich with a sprinkling of fair musk-rose blooms:

And such too is the grandeur of the dooms
We have imagined for the mighty dead;
All lovely tales that we have heard or read:
An endless fountain of immortal drink,
Pouring unto us from the heaven's brink.

  Nor do we merely feel these essences
For one short hour; no, even as the trees
That whisper round a temple become soon
Dear as the temple's self, so does the moon,
The passion poesy, glories infinite,
Haunt us till they become a cheering light
Unto our souls, and bound to us so fast
That, whether there be shine or gloom o'ercast,
They always must be with us, or we die.

  Therefore, 'tis with full happiness that I
Will trace the story of Endymion.
The very music of the name has gone
Into my being, and each pleasant scene
Is growing fresh before me as the green
Of our own valleys: so I will begin
Now while I cannot hear the city's din;
Now while the early budders are just new,
And run in mazes of the youngest hue
About old forests; while the willow trails
Its delicate amber; and the dairy pails
Bring home increase of milk. And, as the year
Grows lush in juicy stalks, I'll smoothly steer
My little boat, for many quiet hours,
With streams that deepen freshly into bowers.
Many and many a verse I hope to write,
Before the daisies, vermeil rimmed and white,
Hide in deep herbage; and ere yet the bees
Hum about globes of clover and sweet peas,
I must be near the middle of my story.
O may no wintry season, bare and hoary,
See it half finished: but let Autumn bold,
With universal tinge of sober gold,
Be all about me when I make an end!

And now at once, adventuresome, I send
My herald thought into a wilderness:
There let its trumpet blow, and quickly dress
My uncertain path with green, that I may speed
Easily onward, thorough flowers and weed.

Endymion was the beautiful shepherd who laid asleep in a cave on Mount Latmus in Caria, and was visited every night by Selene, the goddess of the Moon. He was so handsome, Selene asked Zeus to grant Endymion eternal life and youth, and as her wish was fulfilled, the gorgeous shepherd lived in a state of eternal slumber, smiling and dreaming of the Moon goddess kissing his lips.

My only hope is to keep the dream alive, nurturing its essence every time I cast my eyes upon my darling's face. Beautiful things ease our pain, they give us something to live for: how could we not be inspired by them?

O distinguished John Keats, forgive my insolence! As you can imagine, further revision would not change the state of my obsession. I can only wade through this quicksand-like quandary, hoping to find an easy solution, but in the end I must also come to the conclusion that 'the foundations are too sandy.'

Seven has now left Slovakia. I do not have any more news, not even from Monsieur Gilles. Will they be heading off to Japan? I cannot figure out whether he is tired or not, but I certainly am. These past few months have been intense and incredibly demanding; the full-time commitment to Seven begins to take its toll, exhaustion is in sight, both mental and physical. The end is near, but not quite here yet. There will be so many more days of pain and joy, possession and madness, before my demise finally comes.

New images of my gorgeous torturer have been kindly passed around. His beauty unrivalled: it hurts to look at it. It is too much to bear for both the eye and the soul, joined together in an effort to survive this amount of perfection: I am at a loss for words.

How could I find any? Not after staring for hours at this one photograph depicting Seven shirtless, during a break from his practice session, under the hot sun of Slovakia. He appears to be sweaty, but kind of smiling. His left nipple erect (a small detail that could not escape my attention). Gilles by his side, looking at him in adoration. I search for words, but the only ones I can think of are too obvious, universally spoken by almost every inhabitant of the earth, used to either fraternise or divide. These three simple words my vocal chords are putting together, and I pronounce them aloud: 'Oh—my—god!'

It is an ecumenical truth: Seven is my *God*! Behold thy God!

I can only add that this vision has thrown me into turmoil, to such an extent that I feel physically sick. My stomach cannot hold the little food it has begun to digest. I feel like throwing up. He is . . . Bloody hell: he is to die for! What is the point of living, otherwise? I want him, I will be damned if I do not have him. The most beautiful man in the world, the perfect one, the only one: he exists. A divine woman made him and now he roams the globe (literally), sanctifying the chosen few unable to escape the stark stains of sin all around them. A pure delight made for pleasure, coming to rule this planet. Earth has never witnessed anything of the kind: never again it will. Please, save me from this hell, make me yours. O Seven, I implore thee by thy name: take me away from here!

His latest photograph is so overwhelmingly beautiful I will not even begin to describe it. How can this be possible? How can anyone become more irresistibly perfect each passing day? If this is not diabolical, I do not know what is . . . And then, just out of the blue, after an interminable anguish and an even more unbearable torment, here comes the magic of the divine being that is his mother, the goddess named Marie. She emerges from the darkness to turn even Seven's darkest side into a bright, blinding light. There she is, right beside him, on an ordinary day in the Asian continent. Everything makes sense again, the balance is safe, protected by perfect harmony. If only she had been there more often . . .

Seven cannot go wrong this time, for his gentle mother is watching over him. And I can sleep again at night, at least for the time being. I can welcome his demon and let myself go with him, as a wait for my Master to generously grant me an ounce of his perfection. We are constantly reminded of it, even more so when we look at Marie in those photos from yesterday's arrival in the Land of the Rising Sun. She is the beginning, the one who made him possible, made him real. And today, she is capable of changing things around, this *deus ex machina*,[1] who is the logical solution to all his troubles. No more stomach pains, no more nausea, he can count on her comforting him, speaking the words only she knows would make him feel better, *vaille que vaille* (come what may). And I, the one who suffers as much as he does, but can find no easy escape to a peaceful state of mind–I am happy, even though I never truly understood happiness. It must be something close to this bizarre feeling of mild satisfaction, this transcendent mood I am in as I speak. Soon it will fade away, I am sure, but at least for once in my life, I can say that I have experienced it.

Thank you, sweet Marie, for existing in this crazy world we live in, and for being the familiar shore to set foot on. Thank you Seven, for recognising your mother's universal nature, the mirror image of the divine being we all come from, the demiurge[2] with a mind so pure and elevated we could always turn to for love and understanding. A sublime entity with an empathic soul making us fond of life, even when it gets oppressive and intolerable.

My darling, your cruelty is where my spirit is embodied. The solution to the riddle you have inadvertently passed on to me, is something I cannot disclose; I am going to stare at the empty walls, until I will cease to exist and vanish, along with the incubus tormenting me since the day I was enslaved by you.

You will be on your way to stardom and I will be dead. But at least my insane love for you is going to live on, surviving even death. I will protect and cherish you, never desert you. I am hopelessly in love and in lust with you. Love is what makes lust irresistible, but it is lust giving love a defined purpose. Furthermore, you exceed all that, you become the final creation surpassing all others in this sinful state of mind. Perhaps you cannot comprehend my love, yet you must be aware of its existence; somehow, in some peculiar and unexplainable way, you must be sensing it, as it warms and guards your heart at night. You: my Master. I: your servant. Together, awaiting the bard who will fill the blank pages with words, sonnets and poems. Even though you may dislike poetry, undoubtedly you will be singing his praises. The minstrel expresses himself in a language you can understand, one that sounds like music to our ears, so intensely true and real, just like your beautiful eyes, *mon chéri*.[3] But perfect it is not, for that is only you, the one, the only: the human masterpiece.

As the unexpected summer rain, Seven came to me today, in all his beauty and perverse sensuality. A vivid and astonishing moment of grace mixed with power invaded my room, as I stared at my prince and thanked the gods for keeping me alive long enough to see this earthly angel one more time.

Sadly, he is down-and-out again; when I read his tarot cards, they predicted this downward spiral, so I am not surprised. The only thing gravely hurting me is that I cannot tell him how to get back on his feet, although I possess the kind of knowledge (which is of no use to me) he desperately needs in order to re-establish himself at the top of his sport. It is all irrelevant to the obsession, of course. I am meant to love and worship him no matter what, and a long string of professional setbacks could not alter the state of my reality.

What you must understand and accept is that crazy has many faces, not necessarily all negative. If you only live a life of sanity, would you not be bored after a while? Perhaps some of you like it just that way: plain boring. Not me. Not Seven. We lash out, lose our nerve, find ourselves again; no time for boredom, the clock is ticking fast and we cannot stop. Running, chasing, catching our breath: it is all inevitable. We were born to climb that mountain, and will not rest until we reach the summit. Then, we will slide down peacefully. But here and now, there is only one way to go, one road to travel, one love to conquer. Seven's quest must continue, while I must nurture my insanity and get rid of my occasionally lacklustre attitude towards life. I cannot afford to surrender the will to survive.

Tick, tick tick . . . The clock never stops. Tomorrow is already upon us. Seven's next target clearly in sight. I am naked, stripped of everything that mattered before, because in my world there is room only for one Master, and it is lonely and cold without him. My skin needs his touch, my lips his warm breath; no more games, no more anxiety, just Seven in my bed, my home, my head. Just Seven in eternal bliss and love, in a multitude of forms divinely chosen and shaped, in perpetual motion until the end of time.

This is the love that I know and long for, a single moment of communion with the most perfect being on earth. Seven has to find me, he must seek me out of the wilderness and hunt me down ferociously. I am waiting, yearning, dreaming, but I am bound to be incomplete unless he conquers me. I am the willing prey, and have no desire to put up a fight. Seven only has to snap his fingers and I will offer myself to him: *Domino optimo maximo*.[4]

CHAPTER 7
Seven Holy Virtues, Seven Deadly Sins

In Christianity, the magical number 7 represents perfection, but the Pythagoreans also called it the perfect number, comparing it to the ruler of the universe. The root of the name itself means perfect, complete, satisfied. So, there is no mistake here: Seven's perfection was meant to be.

Are you familiar with the seven holy virtues and the seven deadly sins? In order to explain the mysticism of my beloved, as well as his more earthly nature, I am going to try to enlighten you on this particularly fascinating subject, in the hope to prove the cogency of the moral argument under discussion.

The first three spiritual (or theological) virtues were listed by Saint Paul in 1 Corinthians 13:1-13, and are faith, hope and charity. Is Seven a man of *fides*? My guess is no. Faith is what he demands of others, offering no valid explanation for his dogma. We perceive him as the object of an act of divine expression, and proceed to believe in the mystery upon which we rely, no matter if the supernatural virtue of faith may seem fallacious at times. But I accept, embrace and sustain faith, and hereby declare with no shame: *credo quia impossibile*[1] (I believe it because it is impossible).

To be virtuous is not necessarily one of Seven's goals, though in this case, he does care about other people's general opinion, because he certainly would not like being considered a man without any values.

The virtue by which man's will and intellect will be perfected is hope *(spes)*. It goes without saying that this is something my Master has attained a long time ago. However, dealing with charity *(caritas)*–the most excellent virtue of them all–could be slightly tricky. This is Love, poured in our hearts by God, whom we cherish above all things, as well as cherishing man for the sake of God. It is a virtue belonging to me, I do live by it and my good deeds are generated by my love for Seven. I am the quintessential carrier of charity, if only he would know about my complete devotion, finally giving a sense to all this yearning and desire to love him, which grips me without a break.

The four cardinal (or pagan) virtues are prudence, temperance, fortitude and justice. Thomas Aquinas (a Medieval Dominican priest and theologian) says that prudence (the *mother* of all the virtues) is 'right reason in action', the intellectual judgement enabling a person to act morally in every situation. Seven does not fully comprehend the basic meaning of *prudentia*; he ignores it completely, never asking himself which good action is the most appropriate, because he does not have to, and in all truth, it is a matter of no importance. Unlike all other subdued human beings, he is exempt from such obligations.

Temperance *(temperantia)* means moderation, self-control. Yes, I know what you are all thinking. After reading the first part of this mad diary, surely you must have formed an idea about Seven's personality, therefore the concept of moderation associated with my Master, must undoubtedly raise a few sarcastic smiles . . . And you would be absolutely right: Seven does not care about temperance, and neither do I. This is the most pointless virtue of them all, so let us not waste our breath discussing it any further.

Fortitude *(fortitudo)* is a virtue he possesses. It is what allows men to overcome fear and stay strong in the face of adversity and evil. For those interested in Greek history, it might be significant to observe that in ancient Greece, fortitude was symbolised by the figure of a woman wearing a helmet, brandishing a sword and bearing a shield. This could also be a fitting image for a man like Seven. He has already run into hundreds of problems, coping with the never ending stream of life's troubles, and yet he has always shown remarkable courage in his willingness to attain martyrdom. Has he not been crucified a number of times already? He is a stoic man who has been incredibly brave, never allowing his enemies to prevent him from rising again, reborn anew, just like the Phoenix from the ashes.

Does he render to others what is rightfully due? Because this is the principle of justice *(iustitia)*. He does appear to never let his loyal slaves down, although his commitment to me leaves much to be desired. How long will I have to wait before getting my fair share of Seven? If he truly is a *just* man, he will not hesitate to render what is due.

Man's tendency to sin: do we have to repress it? Would you?

There are seven deadly sins, three of which are spiritual ones, far more dangerous than those arising from the weakness of the body (and I will drink to that!).

Pride *(superbia)* is the most serious one, the deadliest of all the sins, and as Aquinas again states 'inordinate self-love is the cause of every sin'. I do not know whether it is pride that makes Seven such a damn hot sinner, but if it were so, then thank you, Christians!

So he loves himself: would you not, if you looked anything like him? What are you blind, people? If pride is the sin of sins, then Seven is *the* sinner par excellence. And sorry folks, the rest of you can only die with envy.

Envy *(invidia)*, the insatiable desire to deprive other men of something belonging to them and that we covet. Seven has no concrete reason to be envious of anybody, though his detractors are most likely to be extremely jealous of him . . . And this is only the beginning. By the time he obtains world domination, they will all have had their eyes stitched shut with iron thread, just like the envious in Dante's Purgatory.

Wrath *(ira)* is definitely one of my sins. Hatred and anger, yes, I am prone to those feelings and more often than not, consumed by them. Seven can control his anger, although I am convinced that he should express it more openly. Not like I do, because my situation is substantially different; I am mad at myself for constantly failing, for being too weak and insignificant, possibly downright useless. He should have his very own way of dealing with it, as long as he lets his anger out in a healthy manner once in a while, that way it will not fester, and he will not find himself struggling to keep it sedated, therefore causing some unwanted grief (with unimaginable consequences). Ideally, he could vent it on me: I would even be willing to pay for this privilege.

Sloth *(acedia)* is a bodily sin, but I can assure you it is a rather unfamiliar one for Seven. He is too busy living a demanding life, characterised by hard work, perseverance, careful planning and discipline, so there is no time to feel apathetic: ever! The 'uneasiness of the mind,' said Thomas Aquinas about *acedia*: I completely agree. Someone like me lives daily through this uneasiness, discouraged by sadness and deprived of love. It was only the existence of Seven that had prompted me to come to life again, striving to find a meaning to what had been simply a mechanical motion through time. My saviour has thrown me the rope I am firmly hanging on to, as I ascend slowly from the bottomless pit I was gradually falling into.

Greed *(avaritia)*: a sin of excess. There is nothing wrong with the pursuit of money, actually. Seven's wealth is already considerable, though I believe he does not want to simply accumulate possessions, rather he wishes to secure his future, in the awareness of a factual truth: a career in sports is usually short-lived. You see, he is not greedy, just practical.

As for gluttony *(gula)*, the excessive desire for food, I assume he is almost immune from it, in spite of all the well-known delicacies in French cuisine. An athlete of his stature has complete control over excessive food consumption and hardly ever overindulges himself. The occasional celebratory meal might tempt him to put his will power to the test, though this is quite a rare occurrence. Seven's unrestrained desires lie elsewhere.

In fact, our final and most significant mortal sin is by far his favourite (and mine): lust *(luxuria)*. We are both possessed by Asmodeus, the demon of lust, but I must stress the one, meaningful difference setting Seven and I significantly apart. While I simply yearn for him, he is deeply addicted to the unbridled sexual craving. However, the latter statement might not be entirely truthful, as it would not emphasise Seven's natural inclination to be extremely selective and over-meticulous, therefore not just after anybody. Through his methodical selection he succeeds in satisfying his needs, and if *luxuria* is a sin, my Master is turning it into an art, soon to become a proper school subject. What better way to enlighten and inform than to have Seven as a teacher, giving practical demonstrations to any dedicated student out there? Sinning has never been so rewarding and exciting: he glamorised it.

A sinner. And there is nothing more beautiful than that. A perfect sinner is even more irresistible than the rest of them. What you have learnt here is that virtues and sins are interchangeable, pick the one you like and enjoy it to the fullest. I choose lust, to practise on Seven as much as I can (for practice makes perfect, if you catch my drift), and maybe combine it with gluttony (spreading whipped cream all over his body and licking it off like a bitch in heat, as he plunges into me: what a winning combination it would be!), or anything fulfilling an intimate fantasy of mine. The variations are infinite, countless the possibilities, just give free play to your imagination in order to roam this universe and gain the pleasure you deserve. We owe it to ourselves. I demand it for myself: I am a woman!

A rumour goes in one ear and out many mouths, but a recent one came straight from the mouth of this–not too striking yet buxom–French mademoiselle (incidentally, an only child *and* an older woman) claiming Seven had been text-messaging her for months. Why? Simple: it is about sex, his favourite and most fruitful occupation. As previously mentioned, Seven is made for sex; we know his *membrum virile*[2] is ruled by an unlimited desire to relentlessly dominate and subdue the slaves. They seem to inevitably pile up like a mountain of dirty dishes, increasing his personal score to the point that he has now lost count of them: there is always a different one to subjugate, after all.

That is some amazing shit, *pardon my French!* [NB: I finally get an opportunity to write this expression, which first appeared in the *Harper's Magazine* in 1895. A possible reason for referring to this particular nationality could be found in the fact that the French language was associated with things considered vulgar, so it was basically a way to equate French with sex and obscenity, or at least this would be one of the several explanations given.]

Having sex is nothing less than a sublime activity for Seven, he could go on endlessly, never getting tired, never fully satisfied. The energy and involvement he puts into it are unprecedented. Indeed, he should be studied, analysed, set as an example for the rest of the male gender, although it would be honestly too hard for any other man to follow in his footsteps. If he were a porn star, Seven would be the biggest and most acclaimed one in the whole history of the business, for even when he is asleep his stunning member does not really rest. He would be no match for John Holmes, Ron Jeremy and Herschel Savage put together.

I reckon he wishes to meet that French libertine because he has a desire to boast about his sexual escapades; he needs to share his experience, as he cannot let his efforts go to waste. He would allow us to take a peek into his adventurous world, but only to make us suffer more at the sight of his generous instrument dispensing love: the exhibitionist in Seven would just love to digress on that specific subject matter. But I already know everything that is essential, I do not feel the need to publicly explore this particular dimension, and to put it another way, he should be careful. As of now, there are too many unanswered questions about his sexuality and an overexposure (so to speak) would only be causing damage to his public persona. Do not reveal your mystery, my dear Master; let them wonder and ponder incessantly about you. Let the pain of uncertainty grab their souls, as you proceed on to your own path, crushing their hopes.

Giving in to lust is what fills this life with excitement; what is meant to be experienced cannot replace the anticipation, the urge, the physical pleasure. No god or goddess would have created you unless they knew you would go all the way, diving in the erotic sea, riding its waves and emerging like Poseidon,[3] triumphant and overflowing with joy. Only you can offer this amount of satisfaction, and yet you are sparing with it. What you want is to enjoy the power that comes from being the only one, the absolute Master, and that is why you are so sadistic, so cruel. Furthermore, it is undeniable that I am your perfect partner, the demeaned masochist demanding to be dominated. You have seen how virtuous and sinful we both can be, how damnation is not an impediment, and the voracity of our willing bodies has finally revealed itself as the very reason that has brought us together. There is no expiation of guilt, no need to repent for something that was not sinful to begin with. The source of our libido cannot be controlled; we must accept the gift and honour it in every possible way.

Your body is the church where Nature asks to be reverenced;[4] I am quoting the Marquis de Sade,[5] but by all means this should also become our motto. I want to inscribe it on the invisible steel handcuffs coercing me into compliance; I want you to sense the holiness of your body and my complete submission to it. I crave for your sex and renounce my own conscience, I am smitten and enticed, you are guiding me through the path of self-discovery and self-determination I never thought possible before. I ask you to surrender to the call of your instinct, follow the scent of sexual seduction, be wild and merciless, be the forceful animal, fill me completely; howl if you want, drool and pant, rip me apart, but do not waste a single moment and vow to leave no stone unturned. Devour me, yet allow me to sanctify your holy church.

You see, this journey has already taken us to a place of comfort, an island far away from our world, the same one attempting to destroy us, the world that does not believe in us. But I believe in you, my dear Seven; I trust and confide in you, I shall never break these chains and never complain about the pain.

The next step forward is to take the perverted readers for a ride, fuelled by the imagination, in a parallel universe where Seven and the storyteller are already one with each other. We are going to leave reality behind in order to enter this alternate timeline. I am not going to guide you, this time. You are on your own. You have already decided to enter, despite my previous warnings, so do not complain if you will find the following account morbidly disturbing: you chose to be here of your own free will.

I will meet you again at the end of this mind-blowing journey. In the meantime, do not forget to fasten your seat belts, say your prayers and cross yourselves before and after. Deadly sins and holy virtues: remember what I have taught you. Make a mental note of the things you have learnt, they might prevent your stomach from turning, later on.

Lights out now. Be quiet. You, over there: hands off the Holy Bible! The movie is about to begin. Fast forward to the opening sequence. The audience must stay glued to their seats, too late for second thoughts . . . The infernal device has been set. Here we go: time to part ways with your sanity.

CHAPTER 8
The Disintegration of the Persistence of Memory

One morning in May I wake up in a cosy, yet elegant bedroom. I am lying in a king-size bed with monogrammed sheets, when suddenly I hear a voice from outside the door calling me. The name is unmistakably mine: Minerve. Yes, that is who I am in this parallel universe.

I am famous . . . I have done something in the past that has made me a household name all over the world. Los Angeles is my home. I live alone, my now ex-boyfriend James and I never really shared the same roof. He has his own place (he is an actor) and I have got mine. Our cat, Kafka, divides his time between our two homes. We like it that way.

In the kitchen, my personal assistant, a 50-something-year-old woman named Carla, is waiting for me. She reminds me I am expected to attend a dinner party somewhere in Beverly Hills, but all I want to do is talk to my friend, Gilbert Martinez, who is also my fashion consultant. He is originally from Lyon, in France, but moved to Canada twenty years ago, and for the past five years he has been living in LA, where he relocated so that he could place his talent at the disposal of the rich and famous.

I cannot wait to have a word with Gilbert to find out about the last minute details of the impromptu trip he has arranged for me and six other people (including himself). It is a short break to Paris, prompted by the fact that Gilbert has recently got in touch with an old, long lost school mate of his, and has been invited to attend a very special party in the French capital. After recently splitting up with James, I have been feeling rather low about myself, so I have taken the decision to join my friend and fly to Paris with him, clearly well disposed to enjoy five whole days of fun in one of the world's most exciting cities.

I tell Carla I will attend the soirée in Beverly Hills, and bring Gilbert as my date for the evening. After all, it is a safe choice: Gilbert is happily single and an out-of-the-closet homosexual.

'Are you excited about Paris?' Before I can reply, he is already letting me in on his plan to take full advantage of the Parisian trip.

'Forget about that prat! We're going to Paris to shag anything in trousers, girl! You'll see . . . By the time we're through with the city, you'll be saying: James who?'

My feelings exactly! Who wants to remember him, anyway? It is time to board the plane, fly over the ocean and finally make it safe and sound to our beautiful suite at the Four Seasons Hotel George V Paris, located off the famous Champs-Elysées: absolutely breathtaking. Gilbert and I are sharing a luxurious Premier Suite on the seventh floor of the eight-storey building. The other five people in our entourage are staying two floors below, and are certainly quite excited and pleased with the fabulous accommodation.

Gilbert's old school chum is a handsome (what French man is not?) bloke named Henry Boulogne, who has become one of the most successful and sought-after personal advisers to the young men entering the world of sports at a professional level. He is also the co-founder of *le Club Sportif 21*, which is the reason behind the invite received by Gilbert. The club is celebrating its tenth anniversary with a lavish party thrown by Henry and his business partner, and we are so eager to attend it, that we are quickly forgetting all about sightseeing or cruising the city for sex. Although I have been to Paris several times, this is my first one as a world celebrity: the difference does matter to me.

I am wearing my stylish spaghetti strap black dress, the one that has pleats of silk chiffon enhancing my feminine silhouette, as well as matching black stiletto shoes. I expect to meet a considerable number of young men at the club, and I just want to feel attractive and desirable. As I get ready, my thoughts are still of James, who is probably enjoying another night out with his friends, at the local strip joint he has become a habitué of.

The club is located not too far from the Four Seasons, though I suppose the cab ride seems longer due to the heavy traffic in the city. Gilbert and I want to have some fun, but this kind of mood is usually the prelude to a familiar situation involving us and some horny, out of his mind guy, with whom my friend will end up having wild sex, leaving me alone and with nothing to cheer about.

As we arrive to our destination, we are greeted by Henry and his wife, Dorothea, who have been waiting for us outside of the club, sipping champagne and smoking cigarettes. Henry introduces us to Dorothea, then shows us inside.

'There is a fabulous view from the terrace on the other side of the room,' says Henry. 'And the bar is right over there,' he adds, indicating with his left index finger.

'Oh . . . And Gravois has not arrived yet. I doubt that he will show up at all.' Gilbert nods and I ask him who is this Gravois fellow Henry has just mentioned. My friend signs his disinterest with a dismissive hand gesture and instead focuses on Henry's protégé, a gorgeous man named Julien Garoche.

There are toasts, plenty of them, and I do not even remember how many glasses of champagne I am gulping down, but I am feeling light headed and inebriated at the same time. Two hours have passed and I start getting drowsy. Gilbert comes to me to ask how I am doing.

'I think I want to go to bed,' I mumble.

'What, right now? Gravois has just arrived,' he informs me, sounding quite thrilled about it.

'Who?'

'Seven Gravois. The most talented one of the bunch,' he almost screams in my ear.

Feeling dizzy, I turn my head and I cannot miss the sight of this young man, standing under the lights and smiling at the group of people chatting with him. We make eye contact. I look away. He starts walking to me and as he is approaching, my heart begins to race. I am at the bar and in desperate need of some more champagne. I cannot recall who else is with him, I am transfixed by his beauty and immediately drawn to his unexpectedly captivating green eyes.

We get introduced. He asks for a lemonade. (I am not too sure in which order that happens.) He wants to know if I speak French and I say yes. In his eyes, so big and intense, I lose myself for a long moment, something it is going to happen over and over again.

I could compare Seven Gravois to the Salvador Dalí's painting called *The Disintegration of the Persistence of Memory*. The effect he has on yours truly is tantamount to the atomic blast. He shatters and disintegrates life until there is nothing left, not even a single particle of me. After the explosion, complete meltdown.

Lemonade: that is all he is drinking. His lips get wet, and I cannot help but stare at them for a while. We speak words of circumstance, yet our thoughts are clearly of a different nature. The dialogue between us is surreal. What follows is a verbatim report of the conversation between us, although in brackets I am conveying our actual thoughts in the manner we honestly intended to express them. Take it for what it is, an exercise in surrealism needing no further explanation. This tête-à-tête might as well be called: 'What a couple of disintegrated minds can come up with, in the midst of a very peculiar nuclear holocaust.'

Seven: 'Is this your first time in Paris?'

[Seven's mind] I noticed you from over there and thought to myself: wow, is that really Minerve?

Minerve: 'No, I've been here before, actually.'

[Minerve's mind] From the moment you walked in the room, I couldn't take my eyes off of you.

Seven: 'Really? Do you like Paris?'

[Seven's mind] Your dress is fabulous, it brings out all the curves in your body.

Minerve: 'I love it! It's always different every time I'm here.'

[Minerve's mind] I know. And you were looking down my cleavage even from far off.

Seven: 'How long will you be staying?'

[Seven's mind] If I could undress you right now, I would.

Minerve: 'Just a couple of more days. We've been here since Saturday.'

[Minerve's mind] I'd really love to unbutton your shirt and lick your chest.

Seven: 'Oh, you'll be leaving so soon?'

[Seven's mind] I want to take you away from here, away from all these people and have you all to myself.

Minerve: 'Unfortunately . . . Time flies, as they say.'

[Minerve's mind] Your eyes are amazing. Your body turns me on. Oh why can't we just go somewhere, just the two of us?

Seven: 'Tomorrow is Michel's birthday. We're going to the amusement park. I hope you'll join us.'

[Seven's mind] Your breasts are fabulous, if only I could suck your nipples . . . I feel like I'm going mad.

Minerve: 'Will you be there? I mean . . .'

[Minerve's mind] What can I do? What can I do? I want this man, I've gotta have him.

Seven: 'Yes . . . Sure! I will be there. And you?'

[Seven's mind] Please, say you'll come too, I need to see you again.

Minerve: 'I'll ask Gilbert, but I'm sure he'd want to go.'

[Minerve's mind] Of course I'll come. I can't get you out of my mind. You're already in my blood.

Seven: 'Is that Henry's old friend?'

[Seven's mind] Think . . . Think of something to say. Tell her something, anything . . .

Minerve: 'That's right!'

[Minerve's mind] If I stare into those eyes any longer, he'll know I'm crazy about him. Look away now, look at something else.

I turn my head and meet Henry's eyes. He raises his glass and smiles.

Seven: 'Henry is a great guy, very funny . . .'

[Seven's mind] Why isn't she looking at me? Have I said something wrong? I knew it, I'm a fool. What am I going to do now?

Minerve: 'Yes, I think so too . . .'

61

[Minerve's mind] Here we go again . . . Those eyes. What colour are they? Green? No, wait . . . Yes, they must be green. I've never seen anybody more beautiful than this man.

Seven: 'For sure . . .'

[Seven's mind] Damn, she's so sexy. I must find a way to let her know how I feel.

Minerve: 'I really like him.'

[Minerve's mind] He's so damn hot! What's happening to me? I wanna touch him. Stop it! Get a hold of yourself . . . Oh, but I can't!

Finally, Gilbert comes to the rescue. We arrange to meet the following afternoon and exchange more looks, clearly unable to break the spell between us.

'What were you talking about?' asks Gilbert.

'I don't even remember,' I reply. And it is the plain and honest truth. What did we say? Were there words spoken? I thought we talked only through our minds, my brown eyes into his green eyes, his irresistible smile, my perfect cleavage. That French charm, a bit shy, certainly elegant. The list can go on and on. It is unimportant. I am going to see him again, that is what matters.

I cannot sleep at night; the hours are spent pacing up and down like a caged animal. I have him in my head, the sound of his voice resounding in my ears, his scent in my nostrils and the way he looked at me firmly impressed on my mind.

We meet outside the Musée Grévin, a waxwork museum situated in boulevard Montmartre. We are quite a large group of people; there is the seven of us from LA, plus about ten other French ones, all guys. They are a bit rowdy and definitely after some fun time, which Michel (whose twenty-third birthday we are celebrating) has evidently promised them, and is therefore adamant to ensure. Seven has just been dropped off by his mother: the woman must be crazy for wanting to drive in Paris. Still . . . whatever floats her boat. She says she is in a hurry, her husband is expecting her to join him for a late lunch. But her son is quite eager to introduce us, so I get the pleasure of shaking hands with the petite blonde responsible for conceiving and giving birth to this exceptional human being: the honour is almost overwhelming.

She leaves shortly after and I realise Seven and I are now alone outside, as every one else is already inside the museum. He is wearing a royal blue polo shirt: blue is without a doubt his colour. I am wearing a tight black top and comfortable shoes, and took extra care with my hair and make-up. He seems to appreciate my casual yet sexy look because as he glances at my breasts, I can see the delighted expression on his pretty face. There is an undeniable sexual tension between us, and I do not know how or when it will be released.

They call us in, so we rush to join the rest of the group, but are definitely going at our own pace; luckily, the others are not bothered with us at all. He loves the waxworks of Marcel Dessailly, Thierry Henry and Aimé Jacquet[1] kissing the world cup of football (that France won in 1998), but we do not pose next to the wax figures for a photograph. I sense that what he wants is more than just a snap of me standing next to some fake, inanimate men. When we move to the chamber of horrors and walk past the waxwork of a guy tied upside down, we just giggle and accidentally bump into each other. I lose my balance, so he grabs me by my waist, as we both continue laughing. The feeling of his warm hands on my body sends shivers down my spine. I meet his eyes and notice that the smile has disappeared from his face. He just pulls me closer and I cannot help but graze his skin with the back of my hand. He then takes my hand and we find ourselves in a corner of the room, surrounded by images of torture and death. Our lips meet for the first time, slightly touching, but it is only for a moment. What follows is a kiss that is nearly an invasion with tanks and heavy artillery, a powerful assertion of what is going to happen next; an undiplomatic and shameless statement we cannot avoid giving. It lasts a long while, erasing everything that was before, not giving a damn about the consequences. His kiss is just like him: savage, brutal, yet sweet and considerate. A contradiction, many contradictions: who the hell cares! Seven is in my mouth, while his hands are imposing a tight hold on my entire body with no intention of letting go of it. Maybe I am about to die asphyxiated, the hypoxia has shortened the oxygen in my body, I am forced to breathe through his breathing. Air is coming directly from Seven into my lungs. There I go: I can catch my breath again. How long did this moment last? Time . . . Time has a meaning and a place, it has the ability to steer us back on track. Where are we? What is this place? Suddenly, we become aware of our surroundings again, reacquainting ourselves with people and noises. Instant nirvana it was, and it will not be an isolated occurrence, I am sure.

The rest of the guys are waiting for us outside; we clearly must have tickled their funny bone because they are giggling like a bunch of schoolgirls. We get the strange looks and hear them whispering to each other, but we ignore all that and choose to play it cool.

We are off to the CinéAqua at the Trocadéro, and the visit seems to be dragging on endlessly. Fortunately, the guys are famished, so we find out the Ozu restaurant in there is as good as the one in London and decide to pop in for a bite. I get assorted tempura with season's vegetables, a large assortment of sashimi, nigiri sushi and uramaki, white rice and finally the *pièce de résistance*: the delicious poached pear flavoured with ginger, ivory crunch and yuzu espuma. Quite a way to celebrate Michel's birthday! But I am still not satisfied. After our passionate full-on snog in the wax museum, we are back pretending to be involved in the activities of our party, to the point that we are almost ignoring each other. Frankly, I believe this is too much to ask of me, so unnoticed, I exit the restaurant and the whole CinéAqua altogether.

The air outside is fresh, I really need to breathe in all the way. It does not take long before I sense Seven behind me and as I suspect, he is alone. I tell him I intend to go back to my hotel, so he asks if he can walk me there. Walk me? No, I do not need him to do that. He then suggests we take *Le Métro*: yes, the Paris *Métro*! It is ridiculous, of course, we are within walking distance from the Four Seasons, but I agree anyway. *Iéna. Alma Marceau*. Two stops. Childish yet cute. The boy is funny. I am already intoxicated.

'Wanna come up to my suite?'
'For sure!'

He smiles, and I melt like a snow cone under the Sahara desert sun. Here we are. The rest of the world is kept safely outside, cannot and will not get in. It is only me, alone with this monster. We kiss, I feel his body charged with sexual desire.

'*Et le préservatif?*'[2]

He did not carry a condom with him: could he have been more innocent than that?

'Okay, you must go out and find a place where you can get some condoms.'

'I can't! People would recognise me. It is too risky,' he whines.

'What is? Letting them know you are with me?'

'*Minerve ... Tu me fais bander. Je te désire.*'[3]

He whispers these words and I know I am about to give in, because there is nothing I want more than having Seven inside me, and no one is here making me come to my senses. Vulnerability, even when it is only a pathetic excuse for mind-blowing sex, is a weakness too hard to conceal. Someone like Seven can read the signs in an instant and act upon his instinct without much ado. His direct approach and openness are the key to this affair, but it would have been a different story with someone not as weak or as easy as I am.

In the meantime, Gilbert and the birthday boy Michel are wondering where to go and what to do next. The enthusiasm has not decreased a bit, unlike the number of people present.

'I can't find Gravois,' points out one of the guys.

'Really? I don't see Minerve either,' informs Gilbert.

Silence. My friend rolls his eyes. The comments spoken in the French language are easily understood even by the anglophone guests. Certain things need no translation.

Seven and I are ready. The whole world is ready, have been longing for us to arrive and . . . here we are. In heat, just like two mating animals, like the savage call of the wild inflaming our desire to become each other's slave. I have come a long way to find what I never thought it would be there, waiting for me, almost created for my eyes only, and now this is the one thing that actually exists, the ultimate thrill, the apotheosis of indulgence.

Please come inside, ladies and gentlemen. Here is the main attraction. The lion uncaged, the antelope unswerving. Blood will run, and from blood there will be life, torture and a metaphysical death. You can smell the scent of sex already. Just a moment of introspection before the lion attacks and savages the antelope, the fang marks everywhere, the cry of death a piercing sound echoing in the valley of despair.

Let the show begin.

CHAPTER 9
The Sacred Profaned

*N*o condoms. Fine. Does it really matter? Of course it *does, don't be daft. In this time and age, safe sex is vital. But wait . . . I am on the pill. He must be healthy. He is an athlete. Don't they check themselves regularly? One god-damn condom: why didn't he think about it? Silly boy. Yes, he is a boy. Stupid, irresponsible, superficial boy. They never think, do they? No, they expect me to care? And why should I? What the hell's the matter with me? Why am I thinking so much? What's there to think about, anyway? One quick shag won't hurt. I'll take my chances. It's fine, I am sure. Or maybe, instead of rationalising away this potential mistake, I should be looking for a chemist . . . No, no, wait a minute. I am healthy, so is he. We cannot waste any more time. Yes, without further ado: let's do it! Now, right now you goddamn boy. What are you waiting for? You've just said it. You said you wanted to sleep with me, so go ahead and do it. Can you hear me? Are the communication lines broken here?*

My thoughts are completely disconnected. Seven is aroused, yet he is not saying much. What is the matter with me? I strongly wish he would keep on talking dirty to me . . . in French!

'*Je vois que tu es gonflé de désir.*'[1] As I tell him that, I am leaning against the table suggestively playing with a lock of my hair, while he is just staring, a long gaze full of desire. I know the beast is about to attack: I have been waiting for it my whole life.

Again, he kisses me deep and hard while he grabs my

breasts. He stops for a moment to admire them, then flashes his sexy grin. His appreciation is noted. He licks and sucks my nipples like no one has done before. Certainly not James, not that way. Seven knows my body; he must have studied it somehow, because he is aware of things I have never told anyone.

I feel him so incredibly hard against my body and all I want to do is suck his beautiful love muscle. Like any good Catholic girl, kneeling down is not a problem. It reminds me of the sacrament of confession, the moment to share the guilt of venial sinning and get absolution in return. Performing the penance is the least that I could do, I ask for forgiveness before his enormous knob (probably seven or eight inches long). This is my favourite part, I am the queen of fellatrices, cock sucking is an art, and I have always considered myself an artist.

'Je bande comme un fou'[2] he whispers.

'Je veux me perdre dans ta bouche de suceuse.'[3]

Dirty talk, that is right. The boy learns fast. But frankly he did not need to ask, I was going to blow him anyway, although it is nice to notice that the communication lines are open again. Licking his manhood, suckling on its tip as Seven squirms and moans: nothing could turn me on as much. I absolutely love it, next time I should put some whipped cream on it . . . Mmmm, delicious! I love looking at him as he is fully enjoying my knee-buckling blow job: his face is glowing. I bet he likes to eat bananas, because his semen has a sweet, pleasant taste. Is there anything yummier than that?

'J'aime beaucoup avaler ton nectar.'[4] It is the honest truth: I do love to swallow his nectar. And how pleased he is to hear those words coming out of the fellatrix's mouth!

Over the course of the evening, there is plenty of love-making, interrupted only by two phone calls, one from Gilbert asking if I am 'shagging Gravois already,' and the other from Seven's mother, making sure he will be back home at a decent hour. With his stamina and insatiable appetite, this man is a source of non-stop pleasure, a dream come true for any living woman. He has got a fabulous ass, and I tell him so.

'Ton cul est superbe! Je n'ai jamais vu un cul comme ça.'[5] He giggles, but admits he has been told the same thing plenty of times before. Oh . . . plenty of times? By whom? I am possessed by a violent impulse of jealousy. I almost scratch his buttocks in

a fit of rage. He rolls on top of me and covers my mouth with his hand.

'*Quoi, tu es jalouse?*'[6] Of course I am jealous, you idiot. I want to have the exclusive right to his assets and I despise whomever had it before.

Then I ask: '*Combien de filles t'ont fait une pipe?*'[7] He snorts, the way French people do, so I scream in his ear '*Combien?*'[8] His face turns serious as he lightly caresses my cheek and says: '*Tu es la meilleure!*'[9] To the question regarding the number of girls who have given him a blow job, he simply replies that I am the best. Good enough for me.

'*Viens, prends-moi encore.*'[10] I am begging him to take me again: he likes me to beg. With one swift movement, he grabs my hair and pulls my head towards his chest. Whatever he wants I will do to him; we have reached a completely uninhibited stage in our liaison, and if there is any time left we will be using it to test ourselves as well as our perversions. Right now, I am entirely subjugated to his will: he is my Master and I am his powerless slave.

'*J'adore te baiser. J'aime te voir jouir.*'[11] I need to hear it over and over again; thank goodness he repeats the message in my ear, a guaranteed method to get me horny and wet, ready for another exploration of his powerful domain.

Roughly around half-past nine in the evening, Seven tells me he has to go and meet his parents. I am disappointed that he will not stay the night, but I get him to promise I will be seeing him again the following day, my last in Paris.

'*Bien sûr!*'[12] he says. I am happy to hear that. It takes him another hour just to get to the door and actually leave my suite. No need to explain the nature of the interruptions . . . We are so hooked on each other, the idea of separation is already an unbearable one.

I reckon that Paris has about one hundred and thirteen Roman Catholic churches, some of which are attracting pilgrims from all over the world. The first one coming to mind is *la Basilique du Sacré Cœr* in Montmartre, but I guess *la Cathédrale Notre-Dame de Paris* is the most famous and celebrated one. If you listen to the Marian antiphony *Regina Cæli* sung by the Notre-Dame choir, you too will feel pervaded by a strange energy of a divine nature, like the one Mary herself must have felt. Whether you are a believer or not, it is completely irrelevant. These words enter your mind and shape it so that you will never be able to dismiss or deny them. All things Catholic have a tendency to linger, anyway . . .

In Latin: Regína caéli, lætáre, Allelúia!
Quia quem meruísti portáre, Allelúia!
Resurréxit, sicut dixit, Allelúia!
Ora pro nóbis Déum, Allelúia!

In English: Queen of heaven, be joyful, alleluia!
The Son whom you merited to bear, alleluia!
Has risen, as He said, alleluia!
Queen of heaven, pray to God for us, alleluia!

In French: Reine du ciel, réjouis-toi, Alleluia!
Car le Seigneur que tu as porté, Alleluia!
Est ressuscité comme il l'avait dit, Alleluia!
Reine du ciel, prie Dieu pour nous, Alleluia!

But nothing conveys the religious message like Latin does. So, I urge every one to study this language in order to rediscover its long lost beauty, and also its poetry and vibrant musicality. I wish I had paid more attention to my Latin teacher in school myself; I should have been more committed and wise, but of course I thought it was just a waste of time and never truly applied myself. Sadly, only the Catholic Church these days is showing an interest in reviving the love for the Latin spoken word (in my humble opinion, one of the few good initiatives this otherwise obsolete institution is promoting).

'God is dead' wrote Friedrich Wilhelm Nietzsche in *Thus Spoke Zarathustra*. *Dieu est mort*! And Man is dead too: make room for the *Übermensch*. Seven cannot rationalise philosophy and faith, but they both play a part in his life, despite his lack of knowledge of all things intellectual. It takes just a tour of the churches to bring out the spirituality he has been hiding deep in his heart, and the fascination with religion can be nurtured, almost encouraged, so that even he can question his own life and the meaning of it (at least, I like to think so). We are still been pulled by the strings of our mutual Catholic upbringing, but we are no hypocrites, we are sinners and before being able to state that 'God is dead' we must face up to the reality of our (sexual) addiction. Perhaps that is the reason behind our exploration of the path to faith. We might be able to break away from it all, or just accept that we never will. Seven is new to this kind of notions, so I am leading him through the change, hoping even the last resistance will fall.

Église Sainte-Rosalie in boulevard Auguste Blanqui. We enter the little church; my eyes wander around to find a crucifix. I tell Seven I have sometimes pictured him like Christ on the cross, and he gives me this dumbfounded look like I am speaking in some sort of an alien language. Never mind.

'Ever done it in a church?' I ask. He opens his eyes wide, the light through the stained glass window makes them darker and deeper.

'I was baptised in a church like this one. I take these things seriously,' he replies.

'But you're not religious,' I insist.

'Pas du tout!' 13

Not at all? He is such a liar. I bet he is afraid of God's punishment, believes in the devil and knows all the little prayers by heart. Or maybe not. What if he does not care and is sincerely being just respectful of something others considered sacred. What is sacred, anyway? In my mind, he is. Holy, blessed, godlike. I want to worship him and feel at one with his nature, his spirit, his soul. Can it be possible? Can I really possess him?

'Would you do it in here . . . with me?' He looks so innocent, but speaks like a true sinner.

'Of course I would. I'm not afraid.'

He reaches out for my hand and holds it in his for a moment, then gently kisses my fingers one by one.

*'Viens avec moi au bout du monde,'*14 he whispers. I grab his face and kiss him with all the passion that is in my heart; my body is trembling, I feel like I am about to explode.

'I'd follow you to hell, if you asked me to,' it is all I can say to him.

'Then this is the right place to feel safe,' he adds.

Safe from what? I do not wish to be rescued, nor do I contemplate being saved. I want him to take me, abuse me, annihilate me. My punishment? If the fires of hell cannot cleanse me, nothing probably can. I am dirty, and by my own admission also guilty for wanting to give myself to Seven even in this holy place. The disgust and contempt for showing this amount of insolence is the least one could expect to receive. But we are so much alike that he could not feel offended by my boldness, and I am convinced he secretly admires it.

Confession. I want to confess that the sound of his voice alone is made of pure ecstasy. No one has ever heard the voice of the Christ, but I am guessing that if he had spoken French, he would have sounded just like Seven. We want each other, not just in this moment but for the rest of our lives. We have to find a way to perpetrate our sin together, a devious, challenging way to sublimate our passion at all costs. The solemnity of the church reminds us that we have to celebrate our love on the altar of passion, for the two are indissoluble. Love and passion guard our souls, and we come to believe that the holiness of our violated bodies has no alternative means of expression but this one. If we were allowed to, we would consummate our lust at the feet of the statue of the saint, hoping to get a blessing of some sort, but we must settle for less. Just a luscious kiss, nonetheless a sinful one, sealed with the chime reminding us it is time to move elsewhere, like pilgrims of faith roaming the world in search of the final fulfilment.

Our day is spent visiting more churches, until our desire becomes too wild to be tamed that we need to rush back to my suite at the Four Seasons, and give in to our uncontrollable urges.

'Ton corps m'appartient, tu m'appartiens . . .'15 My feelings exactly! His body, like the body of Christ, enters my own and makes it divine too. The flesh is not weak, but strong and willing; this transfiguration involves an exchange of bodily fluids, carrying all the particles of divinity, thus perfecting the purpose of this blessed union. This is why a rosary, bought in the Sainte-Rosalie church earlier on, becomes the rope to tie my wrists with, so tight that some of the beads detach and hit the floor, like massive rocks thrown off a cliff onto an empty road. The deafening sound pervades the room, as Seven pounds and groans with the vigour of youth and the untouched perfection only a pure being is capable of. The suffocated scream finally erupts from this mountain of beauty, as the insistent pounding turns sorrow into delight, pain into pleasure. Holy Christ! Holy Mary! To which extent could we push this unholy union? As the rosary is shattered to pieces, the little cross at the end breaks under the weight of our thrusting bodies. We lie exhausted, morbidly enticed, clinging onto each other, kissing the scratch marks, licking the wet lips, amazed at the ineluctability of this moment. The signs on my wrists like stigmata, as the light of day fades slowly away, and the promise to never break the bond is finally spoken. Heavy words, pronounced like a sentence, they will not get lost in translation. *Je t'aime!*[16] Of course he does. The tyrants of our heart have laid their trust on us. We must honour them. I have to make sure the promise is carved in stone, so I say *Je t'aime aussi,*[17] and seal my fate with a sultry, wet kiss that marks the beginning of the *adventus.*[18] My Christ has come to free me, now I have to free him. As our naked bodies feel the vibrations of the earth moving, the love in our heart explodes, unrestrained and liberated, therefore more dangerous and dark than sin itself.

I let Seven go, knowing we will meet again soon. I am playing host to a precious part of him, something he will need me to return. The blessing of love has been bestowed upon us, its chains holding us together, and all that is required of us is to have faith. The cat-o'-nine-tails is in Seven's hand: I am ready for flagellation. Whip me gently, make me your slave and when our paths cross again, every one will know Minerve belongs to Seven, joined in holy matrimony, for richer or poorer, in (blessed) sickness and (limited mental) health, for all eternity, because not even death could ever possibly do us part.

CHAPTER 10
Voyeurs

I am back in LA. Nothing seems to have changed here, except for my state of mind. Seven calls me every day, and if he is unable to speak to me directly, he still manages to make me feel his presence by flooding my cell phone with all kinds of adorable text messages. His words are filled with passion and charged with sexual energy, he makes no secret of his feelings; I take some comfort in knowing it will not be long before I can taste his kisses again. In fact, his next trip is indeed going to be to the United States.

I count the minutes separating me from the moment I will put my arms around him again, to be enveloped by the scent of his silky smooth skin and the familiar warmth of his body. I am not bothered that James has left countless messages on my answering machine: I intend to ignore them all. In my head there is only room for one single thought and it is not of James, that is for sure. It is only a lucky coincidence that my ex-boyfriend is going to be in New York City for the entire time of Seven's stay in LA with me. I could not have worked out these arrangements any better. Some naughty thoughts are also running through my mind, involving my friend Sabrina and her partner Adam, notorious swingers who enjoy the club life and have tried virtually everything under the sun, as far as sexual exploration goes. These two are so into sex, they have devoted their entire existence to it.

When Seven finally arrives in LA, I am a nervous wreck. The deprivation has been intolerable, I need to get laid or I will die. Of course, he is not in better shape than I am, but I suppose it is a bit easier for a man to satisfy his sexual urges, compared to a woman. The kinky sex toys Sabrina has gifted me with, are a pale substitute for a nice, stiff dick. But all of the above is about to change. I have unlimited access to Seven's biggest asset for the next forty-eight hours, and I intend to make full use of it. Naturally, he is happy to oblige.

Because I am deviously twisted and developing an increasingly sick mind, I decide to introduce Seven to Sabrina and Adam. I am no swinger and certainly have no intention to share my man with anybody, but an idea springs to mind, turning slowly into a concrete possibility. How about being watched, admired, revered by someone else, a passive spectator to the solemnity of our glorious shagging? Just for the fun of it. My friends, the swingers, may be interested in testing us while we give it a go: they are used to this kind of action, after all. It is a thrill, almost like being high, as well as a fruitful way to give our inhibitions a final kick in the butt.

This is a new dimension we have added to our sinful world. It has to be said that at first it was like a dare, a game to play just for a laugh, a one-off thing and nothing more. But now, it has become too intriguing and exciting for us, so we have started consenting to it more often than we had planned to do in the beginning.

The first person asking permission to play this game with us is a rich businessman named G.G. whom we have met through Sabrina and Adam. Quite a handsome, distinguished gentleman in his early fifties we could have hardly associated with anything so reprehensible, certainly not at first sight (though appearances can be deceptive). He has a specific fantasy to fulfil: he wishes to sit discreetly in a dark corner of the bedroom, observing our lovemaking. Seven was instinctively uncomfortable with the idea, so we suggested G.G. would not be in the same room with us, instead he would be peeking through the keyhole, like the classic peeping Tom. But it turned out to be far easier than Seven himself had expected.

The power of our sexual encounter is overwhelming, and as we get more involved in the action, we begin to forget that G.G. is a strange presence spying on us. Our lust and sexual desire for each other are something very powerful, blinding us completely, and we are literally escaping reality altogether while engaged in our game of passion. It is like there is only the two of us in the world, the last survivors of the human race, and all the rest is almost imperceptible, utterly useless.

We are not merely putting up a show, like any exhibitionist would be naturally tempted to do; on the contrary, we are expressing a feeling imbued with generosity and kindness. There is so much lust in our bodies, that it would be just too selfish not to share it. We have discovered the perfect way to achieve that, and believe me, to find an audience has never been a problem.

There is something incredibly uplifting in being watched during sex. Hard to describe, really, it must be experienced first hand. The gratification is immense, the feeling of giving so fulfilling. I prefer to have men watching us, although I know Seven would not disdain to have a few female spectators for a change. Still, it is very satisfying for his male ego to give a performance in front of another guy; his pride is satiated by the dominant role he plays in our little game, and of course, playing the submissive part is what makes it a highly rewarding experience for me. I love being dominated!

G.G. has a fetish for 6-inch heels stiletto boots, so I wear them during our lovemaking session. Seven's imagination provides a variety of options, all involving my body and my shoes. Sometimes he is so incredibly rough, I do not even have to beg him to be; he knows how to read between the lines and right when I am about to go insane with desire, he rips my clothes off, throws me onto the bed and ties my hands, whispering *'Tu es ma salope'*[1] with a voice that penetrates my brain, causing an irrational mumbling of words I am unable to articulate at all.

G.G. is almost in a trance: we must be quite a spectacle. I wish we would film ourselves so that the sheer enjoyment of our hot sexcapades would entertain us, whenever we wish to feel exactly what the voyeurs feel, as they are observing the animalistic act and its shameless perpetrators.

Scopophilia, from the Greek *skopeo* (to view), is the love of watching. It is interesting to notice how many different names are used to define voyeurism or the activities of a peeping Tom. I am sure most people are also familiar with the origin of the latter expression. It apparently derives from the story of Lady Godiva, a noblewoman from the eleventh century who rode naked through the streets of Coventry, in the attempt to persuade her husband, Leofric III Earl of Mercia, to lessen the burden of taxes on the indigent population. The people swore not to look at her, therefore kept their shutters and doors closed, but a tailor named Tom illicitly spied through a hole in the shutter, and was consequently struck blind.

Our voyeurs are not forced to hide behind a door, we are perfectly aware of their presence, and that is where we get our thrills, while they satisfy their perversion. We all need one another, we feed on each other's libido, solemnly devouring the urge that keeps us alive. This is what being alive really means! I could not stop, even if my own life depended on it.

Of course, the original addiction was to petrol. Yes, you heard me right: the one you got from sniffing octane ever since you were a young child and hid in the garage, where Dad kept a small yet easily accessible tank. Indeed, your brain cells are damaged and your lungs will eventually collapse, but think of the pleasure and happiness that sniffing petrol has brought into your life, at least up until the day you discovered sex, and then realised nothing can ever beat that addiction, especially if the object of desire is someone like Seven. The object soon becomes your master, and you surrender your will completely in exchange for that body, the soul of a man's man, wanted by those who can also bear to witness so much beauty and still manage to survive it.

As I am no anthropophagous beast, the saner way to take possession of a piece of Seven is to welcome him inside with open arms (and legs), and I can assure you this is like dying and going to heaven. I would suggest you try it too, but I am way too jealous and possessive to allow such a thing. Just take my word for it. You suckers, it must be hard to look at perfection and not being able to touch it, let alone having it inside of you. Too bad. What do I care? Some people are simply born losers.

I have got myself some nice edible lubricants, one called hot cherry and another juicy strawberry. But the best thing I found are these mint flavoured drops going under the name of *Felladrops*. They come in different flavours: *cerise-menthe, suce-la-menthe, verte-la-menthe*, and *ahh-la-menthe* to 'add a mouth-wateringly icy-hot tingle.' I also love to use a warming massage lotion with a tropical fruit flavour on Seven's divine body, and I must admit that he values greatly my choice to create a soothing atmosphere with a bit of Tantric massage. The lingam massage is particularly appreciated; lingam is the Sanskrit word for the penis (the translation would be something like 'wand of light'), and in this case I am the giver whilst Seven is the receiver. Anything that would get my hands (or my mouth, for that matter) on his cock I embrace with joy and an altruistic spirit. I know what he likes and am not afraid of catering to his every need. The voyeurs might be the ones watching, but only I get to touch, suck, lick and swallow: I do have my cake and eat it!

If Seven is in a wild mood for love, there will be no time wasted on massages or even on oral sex. When my beloved beast snaps his fingers, I am more than ready to provide instant gratification. There are times when a rough treatment is in fact all that I honestly want to get. A brutal display of force which is even more powerful if I struggle a little bit and pretend I have no intention to be taken that way. A little fight ensues, one that I always lose (and gladly so, I might add).

One of the voyeurs has a deep liking for our little fighting game; his name is Father K., and he once was a Catholic priest but got himself expelled from the Church, when one day his fondness for young men was abruptly discovered. A rather attractive seminarist denounced the sexual advances of Father K., also claiming he had been molested repeatedly by the prelate. Actually, these allegations were never proved, however our priest candidly decided to confess to a carnal liaison with a stripper named Sunshine, who had definitely managed to make the sun shine on his dim life, but unfortunately for him, it was a kind of light the Church was not prepared to classify as divine. His acts of sexual misconduct, as they put it, prompted an immediate expulsion from the priesthood and yet, it is quite surprising how he still wishes to be addressed as Father K., rather than simply K. or Mr. K. Old habits die hard, I guess.

I have a feeling Father K. is intrigued exclusively by Seven; the only reason why he came forward to us is that he gets off by just looking at my man's naked body, and that alone would probably be enough for him. But it is undeniable how he also gets entertained by watching us both while he masturbates fiercely, clearly getting far more than he would have bargained for. Maybe today Father K. will be shocked by the amount of roughness and dirty talk Seven is going to unleash on me. Needless to say, I am having an orgasm just at the thought of it.

'*Ma salope, tu l'aimes ma bite? Tu aimes que je te fais mal? Tiens, prends ça!*' [2]

'What's he saying?' asks eagerly Father K.

'No talking! You never talk to us!' I shout.

'But I want to know . . .' he insists.

I am hand gagged by Seven, who is not enjoying the sudden interruption. He turns his head to give him a petrifying gaze. Then, articulating his words clearly and speaking in an unequivocal tone of voice, he says: 'Shut your stupid mouth!' To Father K. this is a clear warning, making him understand he must stop messing with my man. I get so turned on, I think I am about to have a heart attack, so I grab Seven's face, forcing him to look at me, and in a very thin voice I say 'Take me, please! He can go to hell!' Well . . . He certainly believes in it.

We know this is the last time a third person will be allowed into our bedroom. They cannot bear the sight of so much power, the distraction is unacceptable and we no longer wish to involve them. The generosity we have been dispensing has backfired on us, these losers cannot withstand something so overwhelming, knowing they could not have it themselves. But there is a limit to our magnanimity. It occurs ever so often in life that one starts giving only to realise people simply take, and they are never satisfied. Before one knows it, they are feeding off one's energy, absorbing like sponges from the lymph system. Seven and I might be unselfish, but fools we are not. It must stop somewhere, at least before our charitable nature is taken advantage of. This game ends, but it does not mean our thirst is quenched.

As we shut the door behind Father K., we return to the place we were before the interruption. Seven slaps my ass, a punishment for 'talking when you were not supposed to,' and I just wish I could be flogged. I must remember to give him my whip, although his bare hands will do for now. What am I going to do without him? He suggests I would follow him to the next event he has entered, and I suppose I could put my career on hold for the following month without causing much of a stir. I can be his full-time girlfriend, his lover and slave.

A slave . . . He owns me, possesses me: he controls everything. His complete domination is arousing. The erotic drama gets a new chapter every day, more satisfying than the previous one. No ending in sight, because his power is unlimited, but I must fight back the opposition, show no mercy on the little young whores who smell his scent and chase him relentlessly. They too are in heat, bitches with blood pumping veins keeping on at him, ready to steal him away from me, should I suffer a moment of inattention. It will not happen. I will bite their heads off, I will outsmart them. I am not afraid of the competition, but I worry about my man in his lonely nights away from home, giving in to the natural need for affection and warmth, and for someone to hold tight when darkness falls.

James is in New York and that is where we are also headed. Time for a shower. Seven lets the running water wet his naked skin. He is so beautiful and happy. I play the Peeping Tom part and spy on him, observing the intense way he touches his own body; he must be proud of it, I know I am every time I admire its shape and perfect symmetry. I wish I could immortalise this moment, making it last forever. He perceives me and I am assailed by a stupid sense of guilt. Smiling at me, he gently begins to stoke his cock; as I am emerging from the shadows, I cannot help but stare in wonder at his incredibly beautiful member. He stretches out his hand, inviting me in. The tingling sensation all over my body is irresistible: I think I have just come. No time to over-analyse it though, I am already in the shower and without delay, he is thrusting into me as I am squirming against him.

'*Je te désire toujours . . . Follement!*'³ He whispers. Always. Like crazy. Wanting each other. Insanity. Or maybe the only kind of sanity that we know.

He is sweet now. I am transcending the present, forgetting the past, rewriting the future. If only someone was there watching us at this moment in time . . . What a sublime display of lust. Sex is power and we are its gods.

CHAPTER 11
Minerve

I sleep with Seven on top of me. In the darkness of the bedroom, the stillness of the night is agitated by his regular breathing, as I run my fingers through his hair and wonder: why me? Why did he pick Minerve? He has the world at his feet, men and women ready to lay their lives on the line for him, and yet he chose me.

'Minerve: qui es-tu vraiment? Déshabille-toi devant moi . . .'[1]

How could I not appease his curiosity? The night ends and a new day begins. So I sit down and start telling the tale of a woman who came back from the dead to find life again. The story goes like this . . .

> [Minerve speaks]
> 'I can't remember how it all began. A curious child with unusual friends with corrupted minds, playing perverted games. When I was little, I always undressed my new dolls, curiously wanting to find out if they had any genitals. None of them did. The disappointment I used to feel was inexplicable, but at least my little friend Antoine would always cheer me up playing 'doctor' with me. If he got to be the patient he would show me his penis and, when it was my turn to play the sick person requiring medical care, I would show him my vagina. It was fun and quite exciting!'

> 'Although there was never anybody like you, some boys

flaunted their sex, claiming it was the biggest I had ever seen. Not true, of course, but boys will be boys. Back in those days, I would convince myself it was a sin giving way to these urges, though it never stopped me from testing my moral strength. Even in Sunday school there was a boy whom I would meet in secret, a cute teenager who walked me home and shared my excitement for that stupid church funfair. I don't remember his name, just that he always managed to slip his hand in my panties, avidly searching for answers. What were his questions? Every one knows that what you experience when you're still working out the mechanics of sex, is bound to have disastrous results.'

'But I didn't care; I liked to experiment because it made me feel special. I had to be dominated; quite frankly it was a necessity more than a request. People grow older and move away. I started my journey and never looked back. The lovers I took (not many, just the wrong ones) would never last, and couldn't get that deep into me either. Unlike you, my love. Shall I take off my blouse, first?'

'Oui, s'il te plaît.'[2]
I unbutton my blouse slowly. He is sitting in an armchair, wearing only his jeans with the top button undone, his legs spread wide and an air of confidence. In the semi-darkness of the room, Seven's light shines like the African sun. I drop my blouse on the floor as my breathing becomes shallow.
'Continue!' he orders.

[Minerve speaks]
'I thought about taking different lovers. Bisexual men, transsexuals, even women. I wondered about inhibitions and the punishment reserved to those who destroy them and accept sin as the only guiding light in their life. I expressed my doubts, even to priests, only to get more confused and lost. Is this the natural path to self-destruction? Am I following it alone or are there others who can share the burden?'

'Of course, there are always others, one only needs to seek them out, and that's the hardest thing to do. I was often dragged into the wrong crowd, abused by some filthy ogre who mistook my need to be possessed for some kind of licence to express their own perversion or sadism. No one ever understood what I was really after. No one, until I met you.'

'Ton soutien-gorge, ma belle . . .'[3]
My bra comes off next. I bet he is dying to touch my breasts, but his eyes alone are doing the damage. I cannot control my breathing anymore.
'Joue avec tes tétons. Je veux les voir durcir . . .'[4]
I play with my nipples. This stimulates his arousal immensely, even though right now—to be perfectly honest—just a simple look at me will do the trick. He is such a liar, he cannot pretend to hide his excitement. If I am already out of breath, he must be choking.

[Minerve speaks]
'I never loved anyone. The men I had—including my childhood friend Antoine—I wasn't in love with, and they certainly couldn't give me what I was looking for. Antoine used to be wild and enjoyed living a life of excess and materialism. I remember that one time when he was freebasing with his mates after school and his father caught them in the act and grounded him for a month. He didn't care and continued to smoke cocaine whenever he had the chance.'

'Not me: I never touched drugs. Didn't need them, my addiction was to pain and mad men with tortured souls. I'd travel often to London or Berlin, and mostly to Paris to find solace in the arms of a new torturer, an abuser, anyone who'd be able to provide me with that kind of lift. I always kept in mind that I was doing something forbidden, and was therefore hell bound. You want to know who I am? I will tell you: I am a fallen angel. I have fallen from grace into the vile easy world that sucks me dry, gradually turning me into a ghost; I am nothing, zero, a vulgar imitation of what a woman should be, despised by many, sought after only by those disgusting scumbags, who think they own my soul just because they've conquered my body. At least, this is what I was until the wheel spun back my way. Even James has now become a number, his betrayal unimportant, because I've met you and have given you already everything, renouncing my will and surrendering to your power. You are my Christ: this is my very own Second Coming. You came to free me, made me beautiful again, and all that was before is almost like a bad dream that can no longer haunt me. Do you understand what you mean to me? No one could ever give you this much.'

'Enlève ta culotte . . .'[5]
I take off my panties, just as he asked. He has put his right hand down his jeans, but is still looking at my naked body. I desperately want to be the one performing a hand job on him, but clearly his intentions are different.
'Tu es nue. Tu es trop belle, avec ton corps parfait qui n'arrête pas de me taquiner.'[6]
My naked body teases him, he says, but the truth is that he gets a kick out of watching me, helplessly trying to feel less vulnerable. I lose, he wins. Once more, what dictates the rules is the insane desire to dominate combined with the submissive disposition to be possessed. Oh, I am no tease: he just loves to be pitiless!

[Minerve speaks]
'The road to perdition has led me straight to you. If I got lost now, I'd never want to be found. You've got to take me with you, you must love me for all eternity. I've been a bad, bad girl; like Jesus with Mary Magdalene, you must cast my demons from me. Just tell me what you wish, ask me to be all the people you want me to be. My life is in your hands, *mon amour.'*[7]

'Ma belle . . . J'ai tellement envie de toi.'[8]
I want him too. All my life I have wanted him, even before he existed.

[Minerve speaks]
'There was a time when I imagined I would find someone with this kind of strength and power, a man who would assert his authority on me the way you do. It was only a dream and in my mind, I was convinced I'd never find him. I knew

I'd recognise such a man the moment I'd see him. And then, you appear in all your devastating beauty, talking to me with your eyes and your smile, even before you open your mouth to pronounce those words that linger on your lips and carve a sign in my heart forever. Why did it take you so long to come to me? Why did I have to wait so many years, before I could finally find you? Too much time has been wasted, the first half of my life is gone. It's so unfair to be on a deadline. What a sick joke has destiny played on me! All that I ever wanted is here now, in this very room, yet time's keeping a hold on me. There's so much more I want to tell you, so much I wish to give you. I can't rush you, you need to take your time, but I'm pressed for it. The clock is ticking, my life is fading . . .'

Seven stops masturbating. He must be irritated by my vulnerability, yet he has an expression of tenderness on his face, his eyes shining so bright. What more could I expose? Have I not borne enough already? He wants me to go to him, making love is the natural consequence of this intimate soul exchange. If I was not Minerve, but just a girl, any girl, it would be easier for him not to open up; what he wants is to keep the mystery and all I am doing is push him into a corner, where he cannot hide anymore. I do not know anything about him, so I need to strip off the layers until I get to see the innocent boy again. There is no innocence left in me, though. But there is love, he has found it and shown its beauty to me. If I lost it now, I would be killing myself.

*'Parle si tes mots sont plus forts que le silence, sinon garde le silence.'*9

His words enter so deeply into me; like a river in spate, I cannot hold back a surge of honesty culminating in a brutal confession, delivered with a frightening candour.

[Minerve speaks]
'When I was young, I often thought about suicide. I remember how I wanted to die and hoped I would, every single day. I wondered why life was given to me and if it was nothing more than a sick joke. Life has no meaning, it just is . . . Back

then, it wasn't important to exist, all that mattered was finding ways to get closer to the end. I never found them, only sensed I wasn't going to perform hara-kiri, because quite frankly I didn't have the guts. Some people believe that committing suicide is an act of weakness, but it isn't so. It takes courage to put an end to a life, any life, especially your own. Unless, one is mentally unstable or on drugs; in that case, it isn't courage that's needed, merely carelessness.
What? You find this amusing?'

Evidently, he does. Smiling like what I have just said is really funny. And then, to add insult to injury, he giggles at my words. Why on earth is he provoking me like that?

'Négligence? C'est bizarre . . .'[10]
I scream 'Stupid!' and turn my back to him. I should have never done that. Suddenly, I find myself slammed against the wall, his body pressed upon mine. But I am not scared; I am relieved to finally feel his warm breath on my neck and his thick cock wedging his way into my fanny. 'I love you ferociously,' I mumble. His arms are wrapped around me as he whispers 'I am never going to let you go, Minerve.'

Damn right! He can keep me in here, forcing me to remain his prisoner, a convict serving a life sentence of ecstasy and delight. These chains I need, so please whip me and smack me, let me take in life and give out death, to outnumber doubts and uncertainties at long last. I have created my own reality and there is room only for two. Exclusive and unique is this ménage, once the balance has been reached, it needs to be preserved.

'I want to feel you come inside me, my love.' He makes me taste this heavenly gift of love, intense rapture provided by that giving nature of his, a generosity I thought it could not exist in this world. I am so lucky, do not know what I have done to deserve this bliss, but luck never has a plan, it is always random, often touching the undeserving ones.

Minerve is an idea, a hyperbole, yet never a redundant one. She lives inside my head, nurtured by all the things essential to a life deprived of love. What are those things? First there is sex, with all its ramifications and possibilities, the degenerated instinct that becomes the escape route to absolute freedom. Often, there is not enough room to include all the alternatives, therefore sex alone fills the void, almost like the universal cure for loneliness we aim to find but never succeed to obtain. The atrocious sentiment of compassion pushes in from the outside, and physical fulfilment disappears, replaced by the need of companionship.

Then there is friendship, a double-edged sword, risky and uncertain, yet often our last resort. The worst kind of friendship being the one existing between a man and a woman. Frustrating, depressing and emptied of its marrow, this is a feeling that erupts and suffocates, but in a few lucky instances, it blossoms into passion, the ultimate test before the barrier of deception is finally broken. What are friends for? A question needing no answer. Lovers, though, should never be friends: this much I know.

I am not just Seven's lover and slave, I am his counterpart. We do not like the same things or share similar views; we simply complement each other, two magnets bound to be attracted and made to live in perfect symbiosis. I have entered his universe to be dominated to the fullest extent possible for his eternal gain, as well as my own; he has allowed me into his kingdom to exert his powerful influence on this born-again woman whose world was spinning out of control, before he came along.

Minerve, like the Roman goddess, has got wisdom, gained after a life that had nothing to offer. I have become the owl, the inspired deity ready to walk through the burning flames of knowledge, fighting the hostility of the obscene world and emerging unscarred. Side by side with the only man who has taken me to the place where even I can be free.

Sing Minerve, sing for freedom! And when the song ends, the melody is all that remains to carry the sound of everlasting love right to the ears of an angel. Menadel, the fire in the sky, the guardian of love helping us through the difficulties which are steering us away from the love light. The power of love embraces our very essence and we let go of the past: tomorrow is already upon us. Under this very light I sing, my voice once silent now can be heard down to the edge of the world. You have created me, my Prince, and I return to you to stay beyond the limitation of time. *'Aimer, c'est la moitié de croire.'*[11] And I believe! I believe we are life, joy, despair and death. We are forever. A fragment of eternity engulfed in the blackest darkness of the universe.

CHAPTER 12
The Father of My Child

'No one really knows me. I don't allow anyone inside my head, not even my father. The real me is a mystery to those who denigrate, gossip and throw mud in my face. But I am ready to show you who I truly am . . .'

Seven proudly reveals himself, bearing his very soul. Quite a privilege. I am about to hear from his own mouth all the things the world wishes to find out, but never will. The reason for this unbelievable confession dates back a few days, when as I was shopping for shoes in New York, felt dizzy and collapsed in the middle of a department store, on the Fifth Avenue. Here comes a brief summary of the latest events.

Seven and I have reached a stage in our relationship where we are not bothered by all the gossip mongers any more. Even though we are maintaining a discreet and reserved approach to the outside world, we are still very open to discuss the nature of our involvement. We never pay attention to the nasty comments and the ridicule some opinionated people feel entitled to dispense, including my ex, James.

As we were spending some time in New York City, we decided to go out together, something any ordinary couple would also do. It has to be said that the Big Apple is one of those places where there are hardly any chances of being harassed, so celebrity people can enjoy the feeling of freedom gained from roaming through Central Park or strolling along the Hudson River. It was exactly how we felt when we went out on our own, determined to 'shop till we drop,' on one of the most torrid, humid days of the year. [I must also stress that generally speaking, Seven is very supportive of everything I do or like, never complains and is usually pleased to spend a few hours of his precious time with me, doing something different than just shagging each other's brains out.]

So we went out, visited some beautiful shops, started buying clothes, golf clubs, sex toys. I desperately needed a drink of water, therefore we decided to stop at a cosy cafe to catch our breath before plunging into some more shopping. I drank some iced tea and felt less dehydrated, but still slightly exhausted. Seven suggested I would buy some shoes, to match the sexy outfit he had bought me earlier (incidentally, his taste is impeccable). By the time we reached the store, my body was beginning to give up on me. A strange, overwhelming feeling of tiredness combined with dizziness: this is all I could remember, right before fainting.

Seven grabbed me in time, before I could hit the floor, then the security people and the store manager rushed to our help. Someone called an ambulance, and as I was coming around again, I kept wondering what the heck had just happened to me, and for a long moment even feared it was a sign of some serious, terminal illness I might have had without my knowledge. I thought my days were numbered and soon I would have said goodbye to my lover, dying quietly in his arms, in some exclusive clinic in the middle of nowhere.

In reality, I found myself at the Bellevue Hospital in Manhattan, where a middle-aged doctor bearing a slight resemblance to James Stewart, was about to drop a bombshell on me. Seven kept asking if I was going to be all right, his concern so genuine and sweet, it moved me deeply and I started crying. As tears were rolling down my eyes, the doctor reassured us both that nothing was wrong with me. In fact . . . I was only pregnant! That was all I heard, and the final 'Congratulations!' that came out of his mouth. Even his accent and tone of voice reminded me of James Stewart: how I wished it had just been a film!

I told him it was not possible, it must have been the heat and the standing and walking, having no much food in my stomach and only an iced tea to quench my thirst. The doctor would not have it. He went on explaining that fainting is a common symptom of an early pregnancy, occurring when the uterus swells, so that it compresses arteries in your legs. This can drop your blood pressure and make you dizzy. Fine! I had been feeling light headed and all, but this was absolutely preposterous. I informed the doctor I was on the pill and that the dizziness was maybe caused by the headache I got after suffering from a sinus infection. The doctor seemed interested in what I was telling, though he concluded he was positive about my pregnancy and wished to know if I had been prescribed any antibiotics for my sinus infection. I remembered taking something that contained ampicillin: so what? Apparently, this drug does interfere with oral contraceptives. In other words, his diagnosis was absolutely correct!

The fact that I am pregnant with Seven's child clearly changes everything. I do not just mean that it affects my life in a revolutionary way, but it also complicates my relationship with the father of my unborn baby. Of course, he is not required to accept fatherhood, and I have no intention to make him feel trapped. If he wishes to leave and forget about me completely, he could very well do so. I am not maternal and it is not like I am thrilled at the idea of becoming a mother. If this was not Seven's baby, but any other man's I have slept with in the past, I would definitely get rid of it. But this is a special being, something that carries Seven's genes, a part of him as well as some bits of me: a miniature version of us. It goes without saying that as from this moment onwards, the foetus growing in my womb becomes my priority. It has to be nurtured, loved, protected. With or without Seven, this is what I will do.

The funny thing is that Seven has been on cloud nine ever since he heard from the doctor I was expecting a baby. In his mind, this is truly a miracle, almost a divine sign indicating that what we have between us is indeed meant to be. He has no doubts whatsoever and that scares me somehow. No one in his entourage will accept my pregnancy. His parents are going to despise me, his friends will shun me. I am doomed. My baby will never be accepted by the small contingent of French people seemingly so important in his life. My worries are not the same as his. 'I want to lavish all the care on you that you should have,' he says. An offer I could not refuse. Even if we cannot run away from the world which will be pointing fingers at us, we still have each other, and it does not matter where we will be, as long as we are together.

Seven's inner beauty suddenly reveals itself, vehemently surfacing from the muddy waters of doubts and personal defeat. He is about to pour his heart out, opening the door to his world and telling me virtually everything, including what I already know and what I do not wish to find out at all. I have him, he belongs to me and although I did not plan this, he will be the father of my child. This blessing, of which I am undeserving, I accept with open arms and a hopeful heart. Every woman's dream I have grasped and beheld; every man's innermost desire I have made my own, for this unholy union will turn into a trinity of souls, thanks to the unexpected gift of life Seven himself has kindly granted me. He is so perfect, so mine . . .

'I'm not scared, Minerve. All my life I've been scared, but not now. You've made me stronger; I've become like a rock that will stand against the harshest waves, and will never be eaten away.

Ever since I was a child, I've been told I was going to make it big; my parents kept telling me I was special, and that everything I'd do was going to be successful. But they never really took time to nurse my fragility, my fear of failure. And I pretended to be fine, made them believe I was so self-assured it wouldn't bother me to be put under the spotlight.

Many people have analysed me, they have written and expatiated upon my talents, my beauty, my name. Every single one of them had an opinion. Every one had some kind of advice. No one even knew the subject at hand. It's true, I grew up and became more beautiful and desirable; many wanted to be by my side, but they were not friends. I don't even think I had any real friends, and if I did, they couldn't understand the person I was becoming. I hid it from everybody, convinced myself I couldn't show it. There's a place where no one can go, except me; it's right there, in the remote corner of my head where all the demons come to life, and I can't help but feel torn between the loyalty towards my parents and my incessant desire to be free. Freedom I've only found with you, ma belle.[1]

I don't wish to be worshipped, don't need the attention of

those who will turn their backs on me as soon as a new sensation comes to town. I could have all the girls that I want, a one-night stand after the other, but then what? I'll be alone again. Alone with my head. I can't even communicate my thoughts, one has to read between the lines, explore my eyes, capture the fleeting sentiment of need, hear my silent cry for help. What do they see, when they look into my eyes? Can they really see me? Behind the mask of arrogance, there's a man in pain: I want to show you that man. You and my mother are so alike, both wishing to protect and shelter me from the systematic attacks of the army of critics and the dregs of humanity I know too well about. You don't want me to hurt, but I assure you that I can face the angry mob, I'm fully capable of pushing back the enemies. All I ask of you is to love me unconditionally, even more so each time I make mistakes, because you know I'm flawed, even though you tell yourself I'm not. Don't treat me like a precious stone, don't be afraid to scratch me, and don't hesitate to get angry when I act foolishly. Indulge my mood swings, but never give me for granted; fight for me every day, remind me always how lucky I am to have met you, how privileged I am to be the one planting the seed inside you, the beginning of a new life that will validate our own.

I'm twenty-two years old, an only child and a living contradiction. I'm mad, yet sane. I'm wrong, but often right. You know what I mean . . . Nothing makes sense, but I don't struggle to understand who I am. I don't think about the future, though I'm terrified to lose the ones I love. Sometimes I wake up in the middle of the night in a cold sweat, and I'm alone, unable to see in the darkness that surrounds me. I open my arms to the world and get rejected by those who, only the day before, were worshipping me. I fight and I lose, but when victory smiles at me it's my own, no one else could claim it. They try to break my spirit, they push me to the edge, yet I never fall down. I cling onto whatever strength I've got left, and climb back up. This they can't bear to see, the ones who despise the kind of man I have become.'

'There are two categories of people amongst my arch enemies and critics. The first one comprises the 'I've always known he was overrated and full of himself" kind of people. These are claiming that I was a fraud from day one, a spoiled child with no real talent, who found fame and fortune thanks to a series of lucky circumstances. Furthermore, they believe I have an attitude, and that my arrogance is just the result of my lack of self-confidence. In their eyes I'm weak, immature, superficial and dishonest. More than anybody else, they want me to fail big; that way, it would be easy to pronounce the famous 'I told you so' phrase, which makes them feel so good about themselves.

The other category consists of people who find excuses, the "I'd support him, but he might be a lost cause" kind. They don't despise me per se, but they'll never be standing up for me either. Sometimes, they can be harsh and enjoy listing all my negative traits, on other occasions they'll be faking encouragement, trying to trick me into revealing more of myself. Either way, I'll get screwed by both! I mean . . . Whatever I do, I'm facing this brutal hostility.'

'To love me unconditionally is something hard to do. I can be the most difficult person; I can be mean and ugly, even sadistic. But I won't lie to you about my flaws, I'll gladly reveal them knowing there will be no judgement, no prejudice sordidly waiting around the corner. I'm my own harshest critic, after all; you've already caught a glimpse of the perfectionist that I can be, and saw how I never forgive myself for the mistakes I make. I don't look for pity, I demand respect. I love my parents and I love you. I'm in love with the woman, in lust with her body; I'm inside the cocoon, a piece of me pulsating with life, defying all that made me think of death. And I have yet to face death! You, on the contrary, have met the cold hand of destiny and warned me about it; I must keep my eyes open constantly, to avoid being caught in a snare. I can't fool you, not the one I love. You saw me at my best and also at my worst, yet you've never ceased to love me, not even for a short moment. I ask you to take me for who I am, and never attempt to change me. I'm aware this is a lot to demand, but please, do search inside your heart for the kind of commitment we both need to embrace. Don't hold anything back, unleash your jealousy, push me and slap me if I deserve it. Nothing should ever be left unsaid: honesty is the only policy for us. Trust me, even if at times it means to go against your better judgement. Promise that a lie shall never be spoken between us. I am your baby's father, the seed, the spark, the future. You must be cherished and protected, and I'll always make sure no harm will ever come to you or our child. I feel invincible: I can take on the world right now. But just so you know, if you'll ever leave me or take away the fruit of our love, I will die. You are my life: only you could end it. Charged with this responsibility, you might think I'm imprisoning your soul, but I can assure you I'm only trying to prove how important you are for me, and how impossible it'd be to survive without you.

I'm jealous, and possessive. It won't be easy to cope with my insecurities. But I'm all yours, nobody else's. You own me and could break me if you wanted to. I don't have anything else to offer but my love, pure and complete, and my devotion, eternal and supreme. This I solemnly swear! I belong to you: body, soul, spirit and mind. I give you my life, Minerve. Please take it and make it great!'

CHAPTER 13
Nereida

Our daughter is a creature full of grace and genuine charm. She is beautiful, of course, but more than that, she is exactly what both Seven and I dreamt she would be. How can I even begin to describe her? First, let me start with the name.

Derived from Greek *Nereis*, meaning 'nymph, sea sprite,' it ultimately originates from the name of the Greek sea god Nereus, who supposedly fathered the Nereides (or Nereids), the fifty Haliad Nymphs or goddesses of the sea.

When our little girl was born, we felt a wonderful sense of accomplishment and pride. There she was: a sweet, defenceless thing we had created out of love. Even a hardened cynic such as myself was deeply moved by this tiny miracle of a child, who proved herself a special creature, right from the beginning.

Society has unwritten rules and conventions which when broken, may cause individuals to be ridiculed. Somewhere in the history of the human race, it was decided that it was perfectly acceptable for a man to fall in love with a much younger woman, whereas an older female with a younger male was absolutely out of the question. Apparently, it was all reduced to the idea of reproduction, but we know this was not our case. Evidently, a lady can be naturally fertile well into her forties, which defies the concept of a mismatch, but even so, the association of two individuals whose age difference is higher than the norm, is judged in a completely opposite way, depending on which gender is involved. That is called discrimination in my book, but of course, hardly anyone would consider it this way. It made no difference that we were celebrities; it actually increased the outrage, so to speak. The point is that in the matter of love, there should be no rules to follow, every one should be left absolutely free to choose without having to worry about someone else's opinion. It is the one area in an individual's personal life, that concerns only the ones involved. As we get under the severe scrutiny of society, we are forced to raise barriers in order to protect our own freedom and the right to express it; more and more we are limited in our ability to choose and make decisions, as we delegate the task of defending our own rights to the 'powers that be.' It angers me to be pushed into a corner and insulted, but luckily I am not alone. Although my path has been marred by dissent, I have now started sharing it with a man who knows too well about harsh criticism and prejudice. It might seem a little consolation, compared to the suffering we endure as our lives intertwined with so much drama, rebellion and success. But we have been lucky, truly blessed to find each other in the most unusual way, and we are going to stick together no matter what.

I will take a quantum leap into time, for I wish to give Nereida her fair share of glory, which she deserves entirely. Maybe it is a bit pretentious to concentrate the life of a human being in just a few pages, yet my effort is well worth it, because my daughter is perhaps the only good thing I have done in my entire life.

At one year of age, Nereida had the appearance of a little angel, with curly fair hair and deep green eyes (identical to Seven's), although she actually reminded me of a putto. The lack of euphony in this word should not put the readers off; this is the name given to the figure of a young child, found in Italian Renaissance art, often naked and sometimes with wings. The word comes from the Latin (of course!) *putus*, which means 'little man.'

In our case, it is a girl we are speaking of, and she might as well have been the perfect assistant to Cupid. Both her father and I looked exactly like her at the same age.

As the years went by, Nereida grew into a lovely young woman, smart and intuitive, always making impeccably virtuous choices. There is hardly a flaw in her; all the faulty aspects of both our characters are absent, only the positive traits appear to have been taken in by our beautiful girl.

Seven has been an excellent father, a bit apprehensive perhaps, but considerate and remarkably present. It was somewhat surprising, as I initially thought he would delegate most of his parental duties to me; instead, he took the responsibility quite seriously, and never denied his practical contribution to the upbringing of Nereida. She was a happy, only child, who took advantage of a wealthy, safe environment in which we, as parents, were able to instil only healthy principles and positive values. We turned out to be old-fashioned traditionalists, despite the fact that we never even married. Oh, Seven wanted to get hitched so badly: he basically proposed every single day. It was sweet and gratifying, but there was something we both knew meant a lot more than a silly piece of paper: our child. Without her, we probably would have got married, but after she came along, it became completely unnecessary and inappropriate.

We did not want anyone to mess up with the raising of Nereida. Seven's parents found it hard because in the beginning, they were convinced their son was not mature enough to become a dad. Despite the initial difficulties in accepting the status quo, they did eventually concede they were wrong, and were quite happy to admit that we both had made them proud. Our girl was just perfect, it was obvious we could not have done a better job with her.

Of course, the reality was not as cut-and-dried as they had thought. Even Nereida developed a bizarre dark side of her own; it was barely recognisable from the outside, but both Seven and I were very familiar with those signs.

Nevertheless, the only relevant element in the tale of our child, lies in the impact she had on our lives. We had defied the sceptics and the cynics by producing a human being of rare beauty and intelligence. She became a successful novelist, her creative talent widely recognised and highly praised. We never put any pressure on her, or expected her to satisfy our own ambitions as parents. We knew too well ourselves what it had meant to be the carriers of somebody else's dream, and the devastating effects it had produced on only children overexposed to a demanding world created by adults, who had failed to make their mark and placed the heavy burden of expectation onto their offspring. We were perfectly aware of those things, therefore carefully avoided them, sparing our child so much unnecessary suffering and grief.

Nereida did get married once, to a French lawyer. Our son-in-law's name was Stéphane, and he was three years older than our daughter. He was classically handsome, gifted with a splendid physique, and with the poise and confidence of a male model. But Stéphane did not belong to the ephemeral world of mere appearance; he was a junior partner in an international law firm that made more money than one can possibly imagine. Lawyers are greedy people and truth be told, this one was no exception. The marriage lasted four years, then Nereida and Stéphane went their separate ways. She wanted so much to have the kind of love that Seven and I had shared with each other, and despite knowing it was something impossible to find, I really never told her that. I did not want to shatter her young hopes of happiness, and pretended to be optimistic about her love life.

The kind of men she was attracted to, were entirely different from her; she was a writer, an artist, but never fancied the same kind of people. Instead, she fell always for the professional, career types. Except for this one time, when she seemed to be smitten with a fellow artist she came across in Prague, a musician named Dominik Mareček. He was a classically trained pianist, with a pale complexion and dark blue eyes. Dominik was only a couple of years younger than Nereida, but had already enjoyed a wide range of experiences. He had been to the States and resided in New York for four years, then moved to Paris for another three, before finally going back to his native Prague, to perform in the [City of Prague] Philharmonic Orchestra as the pianist-in-residence. Dominik's passion for Mozart's piano sonatas dated back to his own childhood, spent with his grandfather Jan on the banks of the Vltava River.[1] He had earned positive reviews when, aged only fifteen, he had performed Mozart's Sonata in C major, K330, live on Czech television: the critics had dubbed him the new Vladimir Horowitz.[2] Nereida fell head over heels in love with Dominik, but I doubt that he could ever love her just the same. In his heart, I am sure he wanted to, but I guess his music came first, even before my daughter and all the things she could offer him.

Though it had been at the expense of her personal life, at least she could not complain about her career. In fact, she got the opportunity to travel extensively, interacting constantly with various cultures, learning up to six different languages, and gaining the ability to write in two of them (French and English). She never complained about her love life, nor ever felt sorry for herself. The beauty we could see in her went a long way; she had a giving nature inspired by the nobility of her soul, and it showed in so many different aspects of her life. She loved animals, people, books, and had friends in every city she visited; she used her direct experience to write novels that gripped the reader's imagination and fully stimulated the mind. Nothing about her was predictable or ordinary, she constantly surprised us, for she lived to learn and absorb knowledge, her zest for living undoubtedly ravishing.

I look at the life of Nereida Gravois feeling a sense of accomplishment my parents never felt for me. I wish they could have lived to see it, for it would have repaid them of all the (failed) efforts made to give me a direction to follow. I suppose regrets are never useful, because time does erase the past quicker than a bullet reaches a target. Time can be as cruel as the inner realisation of failure, a corrosive feeling that hurts us so deep inside. I am relieved to conclude that our daughter never had to deal with such tumour. Of course, she admits her sorrow over not having found a partner to share the occasional pain of living with. But there is no such thing as a perfect life.

Still, it could have been much worse, like it is for so many unlucky human beings. I have always wanted to make her understand the randomness of living, how it could change suddenly and without a warning, turning our world upside down because of someone else's bad decision. One could be walking a straight path and yet get pulled down, strangled by whatever situation might be created by those around. Sometimes it is simply inevitable to lose one's way, the hope to find it again being the only light. There are no guarantees of success, there is merely an opportunity, but it could slip away before we have realised it was even there.

Our existence is bombarded with useless information: religion, social rules, the shaping of the minds. It is all a mesh, pushed into our brain, squeezed tightly in. We are like zombies going through the motions, wanting things we do not need, seeking a way to accomplish the empty goals we have set for ourselves. The pointless rat race, the waste of energy trying to win a prize in this shameless competition, where our ego is inflated deliberately: it is all clearly designed to rush our lives right to the end. Then, it is over and done with. Make room for the next idiots who will do exactly the same.

As I hold Nereida in my arms and gently cradle her, I can see this is the safest place for her to be. The place where there are no questions to be asked, a simple glance is enough to reach a mutual understanding.

Tomorrow, she will be a grown-up with the ability to achieve all the things the future has in store for her. She will be her own person, so I will let go of my little girl, because she is not mine to keep and her path must be walked alone.

Seven and I will likely retire to the south of France, to enjoy the rest of our days together. Our existence found its meaning when we met and fell for each other; our love blossomed, it filled the longing in our hearts, and everything finally made sense.

Nereida will visit us from time to time, and we will be charmed by her captivating enthusiasm and passion for life. Her smile, the sweet sound of her voice will remind us of how blessed we were to have conceived such a beautiful daughter. We will not be afraid of growing old, because we will be together. And when our time comes to leave this earth, it will not be full of regrets. We will die feeling proud and content, aware we could not have done any better.

Nereida–our very own sea sprite–has worked her magic on us. She has turned the bad into good, transformed two selfish people into committed, altruistic individuals. Seven's genes manifested themselves in all their splendour and contributed to the creation of such a suave creature. If it was conceivable to outdo perfection, well . . . I can definitely say it is exactly what she did. My magic girl, my angel. Seven's most magnificent victory.

CHAPTER 14
Erase and Rewind

The machine needs resetting. This journey is about to end, but perhaps the parallel reality will continue to exist in case we want to jump into it again, should the need arise.

The next exercise consists in erasing the tape, carefully and thoroughly, no trace of the experience to be found. The distraction caused by reliving it, could generate some embarrassment, especially at this stage of our tale. The tape should be rewound, for a new recording must be made, of present and future events, completing the history of the obsession and making it available to all those who wish taking part in the experiment. The memory of all that has taken place should be disposed of at one's convenience, no pressure or deadline to worry about. But before moving on to the next stage, allow me to look back at the moment when Seven and I became officially an item. The reason for this short intermission is to refresh your memory, by demonstrating how possible it is for two people living far away from each other and leading completely different lives, to meet, fall in love and make all their dreams come true, in spite of social prejudice, envy and narrow-mindedness.

Rewind to my first trip to Norwood, for an advertising campaign. Seven is also there, eager to meet me and hungry for love. Somehow I know we will jump into this adventure for real, we will be brave and strong, open to give ourselves to one another without having to hide any longer. In fact, I cannot wait to see his sparkling green eyes gazing upon me, and that luscious mouth of his pronouncing the vows I want to hear. I will then say *oui* to whatever he asks me to do, because my life is in his hands and I intend to share it with him alone. All the months spent chasing each other—after that first magic encounter in Paris—have only reassured us that the only option for us is to be together, finally free to shout the news of our love affair to the world.

Yes, we must rewind this tape, restart the film, relive the emotions. It has to be done! Re-record the voice that speaks from the heart and tells the tale without omissions, leaving no words unspoken.

I am here, on a day of reckoning. He wants me. I need him. We are ready. Let the amorous conversation begin . . .

La conversation amoureuse:[1]

SEVEN   Qui veux-tu être? Veux-tu devenir mon esclave?
[The answer is yes, and there are no conditions either.]
MINERVE   Je n'oppose aucune résistance. *Si tu me possè-des, tu posséderas tout. Mais ta vie m'appartiendra, Dieu l'a voulu ainsi. Désire, et tes désirs seront accomplis. Mais règle tes souhaits sur ta vie. Elle est là. A chaque vouloir je dé-croîtrai comme tes jours. Me veux-tu?*
SEVEN   Je suis ravi que nous soyons d'accord. Il faut que tu saches que notre amour est éternel.
MINERVE   Est-ce que tu es prêt à sacrifier ta liberté pour moi?
SEVEN   Tu es ma liberté, Minerve. Tu es l'amour de ma vie, mes yeux ne rêvent que de toi. Sans toi je suis un homme perdu et tout seul j'ai pas d'espoir.
MINERVE   Mon amour . . . Aime-moi comme je t'aime. Je sais qu'il faut se ressembler un peu pour se comprendre, mais il faut être un peu différents pour s'aimer.
SEVEN   Je n'ai pas de doute. J'aimerai être une marguerite pour que tu me déshabilles encore et encore, en me disant des mots doux.

---

* Honoré de Balzac *La Peau de chagrin* (*The Magic Skin* or *The Wild Ass's Skin*) (1831)

103

MINERVE   Les mots du poète . . . Je vais les réciter pour toi, chéri:

Cet amour [2]
Si violent
Si fragile
Si tendre
Si désespéré
Cet amour
Beau comme le jour
Et mauvais comme le temps
Quand le temps est mauvais
Cet amour si vrai
Cet amour si beau
Si heureux
Si joyeux
Et si dérisoire
Tremblant de peur comme un enfant dans le noir
Et si sûr de lui
Comme un homme tranquille au milieu de la nuit
Cet amour qu faisait peur aux autres
Qui les faisait parler
Qui les faisait blêmir
Cet amour guetté
Parce que nous le guettions
Traqué blessé piétiné achevé nié oublié
Parce que nous l'avons traqué blessé piétiné achevé nié
  oublié
Cet amour tout entier
Si vivant encore
Et tout ensoleillé
C'est le tien
C'est le mien
Celui qui a été
Cette chose toujours nouvelle
Et qui n'a pas changé
Aussi vraie qu'une plante
Aussi tremblante qu'un oiseau
Aussi chaude aussi vivante que l'été
Nous pouvons tous les deux

ERASE AND REWIND

Aller et revenir
Nous pouvons oublier
Et puis nous rendormir
Nous réveiller souffrir vieillir
Nous endormir encore
Rêver à la mort,
Nous éveiller sourire et rire
Et rajeunir
Notre amour reste là
Têtu comme une bourrique
Vivant comme le désir
Cruel comme la mémoire
Bête comme les regrets
Tendre comme le souvenir
Froid comme le marbre
Beau comme le jour
Fragile comme un enfant
Il nous regarde en souriant
Et il nous parle sans rien dire
Et moi je l'écoute en tremblant
Et je crie
Je crie pour toi
Je crie pour moi
Je te supplie
Pour toi pour moi et pour tous ceux qui s'aiment
Et qui se sont aimés
Oui je lui crie
Pour toi pour moi et pour tous les autres
Que je ne connais pas
Reste là
Là où tu es
Là où tu étais autrefois
Reste là
Ne bouge pas
Ne t'en va pas
Nous qui sommes aimés
Nous t'avons oublié
Toi ne nous oublie pas
Nous n'avions que toi sur la terre
Ne nous laisse pas devenir froids

Beaucoup plus loin toujours
Et n'importe où
Donne-nous signe de vie
Beaucoup plus tard au coin d'un bois
Dans la forêt de la mémoire
Surgis soudain
Tends-nous la main
Et sauve-nous.

SEVEN[3] Nous ne sommes pas des saints et nous ne sommes pas des criminels! Si notre amour est un crime, je veux être ta victime, et si l'amour est un pêché, puni moi par un baiser.

MINERVE Si aimer était un crime, je serais condamnée à mort.

SEVEN Mourons ensemble ce soir, parce que je n'ai pas peur de t'aimer et de mourir avec toi.

MINERVE Tu seras invincible avec moi . . .

SEVEN Je suis à toi pour la vie!

MINERVE Pour l'éternité!

SEVEN Je veux te prendre, te posséder. J'ai envie de toi, de ton corps, je veux te cajoler et te serrer dans mes bras.

MINERVE Si tu m'aimeras comme toi-même, je te promets que je serais le seul véritable amour dans ta vie. Peux-tu m'aimer toujours avec passion, souvent sans la raison?

[Seven's face lightens with love.]

SEVEN Oui ma belle . . . Oui ! La passion de notre amour ne connaît aucune frontière; les gens passent leur temps à nous critiquer, ils nous bannissent, mais ils ne pourront jamais tuer cet amour si vrai, si maudit. Notre passion est la seule lumière qui nous guide, parfois une lumière très chaude et brillante, pourtant jamais trop loin de nous.

MINERVE Nous sommes tous les deux comme une chanson, comme un oiseau et une feuille. Nous errons loin du monde réel, dans les temps qui ne sont pas nôtres, mais nous ne sortons jamais des sentiers battus. Le soupir que nous respirons est lourd et profond, pourtant nos rêves des choses à venir sont léger comme un flocon. Et tandis que nous trouvons la consolation dans les bras l'un de l'autre, le vent souffle pour nous consoler, chantant une chanson joyeuse.

SEVEN Cet amour est tout que nous avons, nous ne deman-

dons rien sinon la foi, où la foi a laissé un vide qu'il faut rem-
plir avec notre force et confiance. Notre coscience est libre.
Elle est heureuse et pure.

La conversation amoureuse est terminée.[4]

To be together is a new experience, a challenge. Although
James, my ex, was an important part of my life for several years,
I have always felt we were out of synch, like there was no togeth-
erness, no synchronous movements precisely. Seven has never
been in a meaningful relationship before. That is why I am his
first and will be his last!

I am going back to LA, to my beautiful home where I will
sit by the swimming pool, sipping some iced tea, lazily flipping
through the pages of a glossy gossip magazine, knowing that my
days have found the reason to be fully lived and enjoyed. A
miracle has taken place and I am awake. I have come out of the
womb, I have opened my eyes to see an angel, a man, a saviour.
The hours have turned to dust, time myths finally dispelled:
there is no time. No space either. Try to escape the logic of men:
it can be done. The only existing boundaries are within myself
and my sweet prince; this is our world, our reality, and they both
answer to the rules we have made, no others. In our universe it
is love that reigns supreme, and we are its humble servants. For
twenty billion years, we have been the result of this subatomic
ball that expanded into space, time, matter and energy. But now
we are riding on the imaginary time, rewriting history a billion
times more. It does not take a genius to figure out the equation,
if love is our master we have to honour and celebrate it, beyond
the realm of science and imagination.

If I am Minerve—of whom you know everything by
now—and I was made to serve and worship my handsome
French prince, then time should not really matter. Above it there
is a void, a black hole, and below it one can find the chaos of
creation itself. We need no help from physics or mathematics:
they come from us. Defiant and with complete faith in ourselves,
we have come to accept our fate and bless the day it has brought
us together. We are inseparable and symbiotic, we laugh and
make love, teasing and tantalising without a break, never truly
apart, breathing the wholesome air of our own world.

Seven sought me out, hunted me down; he took a shot at the moving target and then, as he cleaned the barrel of his revolver, he took pity on the fortunate victim and claimed rightful ownership of the same.

'I have a reputation to uphold,' he said. 'I can't let you go. What would people say if I spared your life?'

The doxology I offered did not impress him much. So we joined our lives, no-holds barred, no regrets. Because this kind of love knows no fear.

Now I find myself in this infernal twirling device, spinning out of control, and I cannot avoid assessing reality like I have never done before. It comprises all the different histories, rebuilt under the watchful eye of an extraordinary experience. You might think this is only the result of my own imagination, but you would be wrong. This journey has been as real as life itself.

Yet, I am incessantly forced to bounce back and forth, like a crazed yo-yo in the hand of an unruly child. I could always decide to stay in one of the alternate realities for good, but there are responsibilities and duties in both, people to love and protect, dreams to realise. The deed cannot be undone, I must not complain about it either. Most people do not even get to live one life, let alone two. Instead, I will pose myself this simple question: do I really wish to continue existing on two different planes? The most obvious answer is yes. I am two people crumbled into one self, or what one might call a bizarre, unprecedented reinterpretation of the Siamese twinning. I could not be separated from my other twin. I face the usual dilemma: should I keep both alive, or free just one and kill the other? (This digression is perhaps unnecessary, at this point of my tale . . .)

Apart from the relevant doubts this situation has created, there is one certainty: my love for Seven remains unchanged and unchallenged in either universe. There is no turning back the clock, though, the process is irreversible; forward I go, right to the end, unalloyed and unbending. I am getting off in a minute, but before returning to the initial point, I want to make sure Seven will keep me in his thoughts. So I kiss him. One kiss can carry all that knowledge, and yet never bend under the weight of the responsibility. Just one last look into his dreamy green eyes, a silent sigh and a tender caress, a tiny gesture imprisoning the love beyond the boundaries of our universe. The lonesome traveller now ready to leave.

He gives me one last inquisitive look and I smile.

'I think you're luminous,' I say. Then I walk away, leaving the peace of the moment to enter the space in which the centrifugal force of time is sending me.

The tape has been erased, then rewound. I bury my head under the pillow. The screeching sound of the alarm clock is so unpleasant to the ear, it almost makes it bleed. There are no monogrammed sheets, no voices calling me from out the door. I am back. I am awake. My first thought is: *Where is Seven today?*

CHAPTER 15
A World Apart

Seven is sick again. Even on his home soil, he feels abandoned, misunderstood and unfairly criticised by everyone. If there is one thing he despises, it is criticism. He never was one to accept it without a fight; his strong rejection perhaps due to his pride, although his reasons were justified by the bad faith of his detractors, always willing to dig deep until they find some ridiculous excuses to treat him like dirt. No matter if at times he has been sincerely hurt, both physically and psychologically, and therefore unable to fulfil their expectations.

The latest *illness* comes as no surprise to me. I was indeed expecting it. The worst part, though, is that for the next three weeks I will be deprived of Seven altogether. No interviews, no photos or nice videos: complete lack of news. Darkness will surround my cosmos once again, for he is the light and when he is gone, he takes life away from me.

I bet he will have plenty of fun now. He has been looking forward to this break, I know it. All this time, the one thought in his head has been to go away, shut the world outside and become an ordinary human being for a short while. The slaves will make sure a little bit of the extraordinary gets its just reward. One cannot expect Seven to give it all up, after all. It would be impossible, in fact. Even if he wanted to, he would never be able to get rid of himself: he was born perfect, and they are certainly not blind.

I feel ugly. I am ugly.

Life is truly a joke. It is over too soon and for some, it has never really begun. I am one of them, I suppose.

Maybe I love Seven so intensely because he has been blessed with so much, never had to face self-pity or regret. For what I know, his simple mind does not even allow such empty feelings.

But I am not complaining. He is what he is and I adore him just the same. The only sad realisation is that he will never know about all this: the diary, the story, the obsession. The most beautiful things are born out of obsession, someone once said to me. Yes, beautiful things born out of utter ugliness: that is the miracle of Seven.

I love him, yet there is nothing pleasant about it. My feeling is a cancer devouring me piece by piece, and there is no way out either—as stated plenty of times before—because this is despair, however enticing and uplifting it might be, it still has a destructive and final effect on me. My morbid thoughts reveal the monstrous side of my conscience, no one should ever make terms with. A possession can be dangerous for others as well as for ourselves, so it would be better to hide the monster and wait for the night; the door must be locked, the lights diligently turned off. In the complete darkness, demonic shadows are dancing wildly, celebrating their glorious moment of victory, while I cannot help myself but wish there was another way to deal with my fiendish dependence. Instead, I am none other than an eager spectator attending this demonic, grotesque spectacle.

I will definitely be seeing Seven tonight, thanks to the miracle of modern technology.

The new year has just begun, and this will be the first glimpse of him after a long, complicated wait, during which I was starving for a piece of my prince, but was inevitably denied one. That is also why I hate the holidays. They take time away and never return it; they put me in an awkward position, where I have to pretend to care, despite knowing I have stopped caring a long time ago. One can easily detect the irony of it all; a time of the year when even cynics, such as myself, have to comply to the meaningless routine. It may be just a phone call, or a special feast, or a casual encounter, yet we all have to submit to the unspoken rule. Pretend we care: pretence is scary!

I doubt Seven has ever been worried about this. His parents must have coached him well; they must have instructed him to behave in the proper manner, and it is quite obvious he has never failed them since. Even though he is no longer a child, he still has a trick or two up his sleeve. A deceiver is especially at ease during this time of the year. It is the curse cast upon us by the Christian world, no one escapes it; one way or the other, we all become victims (some of us more willingly than others).

Now that Seven is on the other side of the earth from where I am (and right there he will be staying for at least a month), I wonder whether this new year will bring me any gifts at all. When I encountered my demonic master, I certainly had not predicted such an event would ever take place. Yet, something always happens, an accidental episode turning the light on at the end of my tunnel, only to switch it off abruptly shortly after. There can be no alternative for people like me but to accept the naked truth, although I am not completely sure there are any lost souls going through the very same ordeal, day in and day out. Probably not, but one can always hope to find another deranged mind to lean on.

I made the reasonable choice of not watching Seven in action last night, unlike the morning before, when I had the pleasure of seeing him for the first time in this new year. How on earth was I able to sleep, knowing I could have seen his beautiful face again? The fatigue made the most of my night, but sadly I was not granted a single dream of my handsome torturer.

For the past week, I have been able to see Seven every other day. The first time I stayed up late, and as I was drifting into a dreamlike state, it was almost as if I could hear his voice and touch him, so real he appeared to me. I could not tell whether I was watching him at his very best, or if it was only my imagination deceiving me like that. But he was real, in all his splendour, his perfection, and I enjoyed every minute of the experience until yesterday, when it almost hurt to see him. It must be that aura of confidence, the positive attitude he seems to have finally found. The more I am saddened by my own failing existence, the happier he appears to be with his glorious rebirth. I am hurt, yes, but also proud that he is finding his way into the world, showing he can be up with the best and never quit a fight.

That is my man, my Seven, my eternal anguish and ecstasy.

And now, for many more days he will disappear again. I must wait and be patient, no matter how difficult this is. I suffer in silence, my pain unheard, my solitude building up more walls around me. Seven's pain is different than mine, and can be eased in the most obvious way; he knows nothing about the nightmares, cannot be tormented by the same silent scream of terror I hear every single day of my life. He is lucky, blessed with perfection, cursed only by the mediocrity of the rest of us: he is out of our league. Searching for the next thrill, he is learning fast to control his power, I can see it clearly now. The new year has offered Seven an unforeseen opportunity to use his infallible weapon yet again, with the sole purpose of luring more slaves willing to sacrifice themselves for him.

Half of the world divides us right now, but as we speak, he is boarding a plane, possibly bound for France. Nevertheless, it is not just the distance that separates us; in reality, no matter how close to me he may be, we will always be poles apart. I am invisible, he could never see me, only I can explore his soul and mind, and even write about it. There are stars in the sky that are closer than the two of us. It is bloody dreadful being forced to share him with so many others: I am not an altruist! At the constant risk of sounding unkind, I push the meaningless slaves away, wishing they would bite the dust, crying out in pain as they slither along the ground. If it were up to me, I would show no mercy and finish them off with my own two hands, but I am no ringmaster. Furthermore, Seven is convinced he needs them. I suppose he does, to a certain extent; he occasionally rewards his sycophant subjects with a few sweet morsels of hope, and they revel in their bafflement. I guess there is only one proper way to settle the dispute, a solution serving effectively both uncompromising factions; for the sake of my maker I will have to accept their existence, as there is no other choice but to tolerate their foul stench for many years to come.

Tonight, for instance, they were out just like jackals, like salivating vultures ready to feast upon the flesh of my Master, defeated once again after yet another unsuccessful battle. They do believe they can help, but this is pure delusion. It would be simply impossible for them to provide any comfort to the dispirited warrior. The previous aura of confidence has quickly

113

disappeared: even I did not expect such poor results. Again, another long wait is in sight, perpetrating a senseless agony that I cannot fully escape. But I smile, for today Seven and I were joined in defeat, so I feel less lonely because of him. Maybe I am truly crazy, the signs of madness are too evident to deny, and even though this sad tragedy leaves no room for false hope, I still have a grin on my face. Who knows what else we will find, marching on like little soldiers down the path leading to the end of our earthly journey. No one can tell what will happen tomorrow, this goes for people of all ranks and classes, and it most certainly does include me. My perceptions are confused, led astray by that beautiful smile of his. The innermost desire solidly untouched, awaiting the merciful demon to grant a single moment of release. No one knows what the future will bring, but maybe–just maybe–it will be my turn to shine.

I am sickened by the constant gossiping of those stupid girls. It is time to push my masochism away and avoid reading all that nonsense: it does not help my illness. In less than two days, Valentine's Day will be upon us again. *Quelle torture!*[1] It will be the worst time of the year to reflect on Seven's life and achievements. The reason being the realisation I am not a part of it all. Call me selfish (which I am), but if there is a moment to have him close and present, it would certainly be this one. I hope Seven is not too mawkish, though I can tell that with a little bit of coaxing he can get anything he wants from anyone (especially women). He has been spoilt rotten by his parents, has learnt all the right tricks: he is a receiver not a giver at the best of times. Love him or loathe him, this man has always had a personal style and a discerning element setting him apart from the rest of us. It is beyond doubt that he is never cowed by the latest fashion or trend, this is a pure individualistic man unwilling to satisfy other people's demands. His ego, which has hitherto been only fed by fans and close friends, has suddenly become the subject of debate among perfect strangers. Oddly enough, this sudden intrusion affects someone who, as a rule, does not even allow a short peek into his private life.

      How different and far apart are we really? It is ironic to concede that even two people like us could theoretically have a relationship of some sort, though in fact this situation imposes a different conclusion. It is sad as well as true, I am not deluded: I can still tell the difference between what is real and what is not. But this stupid Valentine's Day could have been different, better, perhaps even fruitful. Instead, it is just like any other day . . . Only worse!

Whenever Seven is in France, I feel somehow relieved; he is within reach, nonetheless completely unattainable, and that is a fact. When one has certainties, however depressing they may seem, one can easily accept the living hell and suffer the consequences of it without turning a hair. I have learnt to live like this many years ago, when it was premature to predict future events, and yet I already knew I was going to end up a failure. It is not out of self-deprecation that I am pronouncing these words, I am proud of my failures just as much as ordinary people are proud of their accomplishments. After all, it takes a rather special person to fail so badly, so often and from a very early age. It is a talent, a gift I do not intend to deprive myself of: what else would I have to show for, otherwise? No, a disaster is better than nothing at all, and my specialty is plain for everybody to see: disasters play in an infinite loop. It is like being left on the starting blocks after the starter has fired the gun; you stay there, then begin building your own existence right on the assigned lane number, at no additional cost. Well, to tell the truth, even standing still and looking like an ugly scarecrow is not completely free (but that is another story). I know exactly what every poor sod feels, every loser on earth, every low-life scum: they all feel paralysed. Once in a while, someone like Seven (though not as perfect, in most cases) comes along, and suddenly the stillness seems to end, offering hope for a better life. But it never lasts; soon enough, we realise we have not actually moved an inch, and so the tragedy continues to be. There is always a new one every day, to take us to the next journey full of sorrow, while the cynical charade of the brief moment on earth called life, gets more reruns than a bad soap opera, ensuring more thrills and drama to an eager, ferocious audience. Spectators are also actors in this comically distorted show, where tears are never dry, the applause kindly dispensed, for this spectacle needs no rehearsal once it gets on the way. Whenever a curtain is lowered, another one is raised, as the trained animals that we are compete against each other. Enjoy it while it lasts, there is no call back, no second chance. The pain is real, the blood quite thick, the paradox rigorously true.

CHAPTER 16
The 7 Slaves of Seven

Definition of the word slave according to the Merriam-Webster Dictionary:[*]

Pronunciation: \'slāv\
Function: noun
Etymology: Middle English *sclave*, from Anglo-French or Medieval Latin; Anglo-French *esclave*, from Medieval Latin *sclavus*, from *Sclavus* Slavic; from the frequent enslavement of Slavs in central Europe during the early Middle Ages.
Date: 14th century
1 : a person held in servitude as the chattel of another
2 : one that is completely subservient to a dominating influence
3 : a device (as the printer of a computer) that is directly responsive to another . . .

Definitions one and two are spot on. I am a person held in servitude as the chattel of Seven, but mostly I am completely subservient to the dominating influence of my Master. There are others in a similar situation, and I shall tell you all about them. I have selected seven prototypes of slaves to put on display for your

---

[*] By permission. From *Merriam-Webster's Collegiate® Dictionary, 11th Edition*©*2010* by Merriam-Webster, Incorporated (www.Merriam-Webster.com).

evaluation, and I am leaving myself out for the following reasons.

First of all, my status is not exactly the same as theirs; I am mentally ill, I live in a reality that serves the purpose of keeping me alive by the skin of my teeth. My obsession with Seven is the main ingredient to this recipe for disaster I have exclusive right to. Despite being a privilege, this is also a terminal condition, leading to nothing but the end of my existence, and in fact, I have already started coming apart. As you can gather, I stand out like a sore thumb.

Furthermore, I do not see my Master with the same eyes as those people do; I see the demon in all its spellbinding power, and have a clear understanding of what is hidden behind those seemingly innocent green eyes. That is why I have been enslaved on a higher level and it would be too scary for Seven himself coming to terms with this concept. I love him dearly, but I know he is not that bright!

Having stated the premises to this argument, I can now proceed to give you a few examples of the women (and a man) who have fallen for my Prince; seven people out of thousands sharing with each other, on a regular basis, the delight of his existence. These carefully selected specimens are perfect models of the so-called fans, recruited willy-nilly by Seven during the course of the past few years. They are all equally intrigued by him, despite being very different in cultural background, social standing, age, nationality, sex, and last but not least, personality.

The meeting point for all of them is a public forum dedicated to Seven, where after accepting some basic rules, this particular cyber-community joins in to analyse, discuss and reflect on every aspect of the life and career of the semi-god of their choice. They are:

Mrs. Guthrie–aka the desperate housewife
Miss Kiki–aka the American globe trotter
Miss Linda–aka Aussie girl
Mademoiselle Primevère–aka the French maid
Mademoiselle Manu–aka the French teenage fan
Mr. Lee–aka the man in charge
Lola–aka the beauty queen

Mrs. Guthrie earned herself the title of 'desperate housewife' because that is exactly what she is. I would say she is in her late twenties, possibly early thirties, married to a man who works a lot and does not have enough time to spend on her and the children, hence she is bored stiff with the household chores, as well as sick and tired of engaging herself in nothing more than a meaningless routine. Her life is so dull and uneventful, it even beats mine! So, the perfect place to let go of her frustrations is the virtual space where she can join the collective fantasy about a young, handsome man who is exactly the opposite of her own husband, a fantasy so real it makes her day . . . every single blasted day!

She is desperate for love, but she is also witty and intelligent, quite charming in several ways. Although I find that I can definitely relate to her on so many different levels, I am also convinced I could never be her friend. All and all, we are after the same thing, something I do not wish to share, and that is not negotiable. Still, she is possibly one of the most non-threatening of Seven's slaves, though she is smart, a quality I cannot afford nor make the mistake to underestimate.

On the other hand, Miss Kiki–also known as the American globe trotter, for her roaming spirit and her passion for the groupie lifestyle–does not have any time to waste on boring chores. She is quite young and pretty, and has posted several pictures of herself on line, as her vanity is enormous and her need to be complimented almost insatiable.

This little gem has also been able to meet Seven, on more than one occasion. I do not know exactly what he makes of her, my friends. I can tell that he is very pleased to see her, accepting her gifts with open arms, appearing always happy to pose for a photo or spend a few minutes in her pleasant company. Although he is a born philanderer, it is very unlikely that he might want to sleep with her, as I am sure he does not perceive her as someone to be intimate with, and for a rather simple reason: she is younger than he is. Seven prefers older women, by his own admission, so there is nothing exciting about those girls, except maybe the way they inflate his ego. He loves being treated like a special person, adored and admired like a true god. Still, he would find far greater satisfaction in taking to bed someone like Mrs. Guthrie, as long as she is attractive, of course (being a man of his generation, Seven has no particular interest in ugly women, no matter how available they may be).

Our Miss Kiki is very devoted to him and under the (false) impression that at each surprising encounter, he is always giving her the eye. But she knows nothing about the drama, the pain, the utter despair that are so vital to the survival of the obsession. The negative forces cannot be discarded: they come with the territory. Only a true believer knows the depths of the chasm; only a perfect victim accepts the extent of the torment. Our sweet Kiki is neither.

Nor is Miss Linda, the fun-loving, troublemaking Aussie girl. She is primarily a liar, who delights herself in spreading unsubstantiated rumours about Seven, and secondarily a lascivious idiot, the result of a severe lack of parenting and an insufficient level of education, or what one might call 'a perfect example of our self-inflicted societal collapse.' (NB: I am self-quoting here!)

Miss Linda claims she has actually slept with Seven at least once, but has failed in reality to provide hard evidence of the occurrence. In addition to the infantile behaviour, the thing that irritates the most about her is the way she makes a mockery of our feelings by blatantly flaunting her sexuality. Although I have never engaged in a conversation with this moron, I have come to the conclusion that she is an attention seeker who would do or say anything in order to get an audience. So far, no one has bought her stories, and I predict that no one ever will. Miss Linda is a loud mouth and a ridiculous little girl. In a nutshell . . . Pathetic!

For Mademoiselle Primevère (aka the French maid), Seven is merely a pastime, a pleasant distraction from a life otherwise extremely busy and lived to the fullest. This one has no time for useless occupations; she is a very modern woman, a socialite and a fashionable lady. I call her the French maid because I literally picture her wearing the costume of the same name, while engaging in some raunchy activities with the occasional lover. I do not know how old she is, I reckon she could be in her mid-twenties, but I imagine her being sophisticated, elegant and stylish like only French women can be. These types, though, have a soporific effect on Seven; his countrywomen raise very little interest in him, maybe because they are too predictable.

As for Mademoiselle Manu, our little girl wonder, she is still too young to be making a lasting impression on my Master's life. None of these slaves have a real impact anyway, as he does not care about the virtual world of followers. He loves to be adored, oh yes, but prefers the worshippers to be made of . . . flesh and blood. We are almost insignificant in his eyes, so he barely acknowledges our existence. When it comes to giving his devotees some recognition, there is not a soupçon of mercy one could find in him. Manu must know it in her heart that her love and admiration are wasted on such a cruel man. But she has the enthusiasm of youth, an almost religious fervour burning in the soul of a French teenager, with many interests and hobbies, and a large group of like-minded friends to rely on. Funny how she can communicate so easily with Mrs. Guthrie, accepting her advice and maternal attention, as if there was a genuine friendship between them. She is kind of sweet, but as hopeless as the rest of us, nonetheless.

Mr. Lee is the only male slave in this particular selection. He is of Asian origins and has met Seven quite a few times. His interest is purely professional, but I am very fond of him because he provides us with photos and information at a constant rate. I do not think he enjoys the female chit-chat, therefore his presence is always discrete and a bit formal. He would by far prefer to analyse Seven's progress and results with a critical approach, unlike us, who have become unhinged, and cannot quite separate the profession from the man.

One girl unable to make that important distinction is our charming Lola, universally recognised as a true beauty queen. Beautiful she is, Seven himself could not help but notice her, after meeting her a couple of times. If there were only one of us with a real chance of making it to the next stage, it would be Lola. She has got what it takes to get him into bed, she could definitely try if she wanted to, but I have doubts she ever will. Despite being pretty and available, she lacks the confidence it would take to make the qualitative leap with Seven. Also, if he really were interested in her, he would have taken her already. My Master is not one to shy away from an opportunity served on a silver platter.

There are also slaves who have taken a different approach, not wanting to be considered subservient to Seven's influence, and yet they could not escape their condition. One example is someone that I will call *Lint*, an individual who used to love Seven, and has done so for many years. *Lint* has expressed admiration and praise not only to the athlete but also to the man (no one can escape that, after all), only to realise at some point, that Seven has done things differently, too differently than expected, therefore upsetting and frustrating other people's expectations. For *Lint* in particular, this has been unbearable, so the criticism and insults have started pouring down as thick as hail. Some people are enslaved even by Seven's failures, and that has to be considered quite unique in this world. Can anyone find me another man who can show an ability to gather such a crowd of worshippers, some of which are imprisoned by a sentiment so distant from that of love and adoration? I challenge you to name me just one person who shares my Master's gift. Think hard and come up with an answer before the end of this sentence. *(Bursting with laughter.)*

I assume that no other slave is like me, but at least we all have one thing in common (besides our love for Seven); each and every one us is perfectly aware he is much more insightful and complex than he first appears to be. In fact, his complexity is such that not even his parents can truly say they can read into it; the vain attempts of making some sense of the apparent mess reigning in his head, becomes each time more embarrassing. But that is not all. One side of Seven–his darkest, most perilous one–remains uncharted territory for the majority of us, and our tormented slavery is furthermore inexplicable because of that. How could anyone in his right mind ever become a possession of a man who might, at any given moment, erupt with an explosive volcanic energy, destroying himself alongside the rest of us? It is hard to tell, but in accepting our status we are allowing ourselves to be dominated, our free will domesticated and tamed by this superior being. Perhaps, I am the only one aware of the process, while the others cannot perceive themselves as mere objects.

My addiction makes him stronger, and I wish he could

use that strength to communicate with me. Sadly, there is no such thing as telepathy, or any other kind of communication between minds other than by the known senses. And I doubt that Seven possesses a capability to use even the spoken language in a fruitful way, giving his cultural deficiency and lack of proper schooling. But, on a rather subtle level, he can be incredibly communicative, to the point of saying too much and running the risk of being completely misinterpreted. I would love to teach him those skills needed to perfect the art of eloquence, so that he could astonish his detractors and shut them up once and for all. It will never happen, I know, although it is a positive thought to toy with, in spite of Seven's renowned ignorance. Ignorance is bliss, they say. I disagree. 'The only good is knowledge and the only evil is ignorance,' stated Socrates. Not that my prince is evil, only cruel perhaps; yet, if he could ever become learned and erudite, he would increase the goodness of his heart and understand himself more. He would proceed with the recantation of all the statements that have often contributed to ridicule and humiliate him, and finally he would pick out only the slaves worthy of the highest praise, inviting them to sit by his side to serve him as he deserves to be served. Amongst them, I would be the chosen one, the sole individual to count on and trust unconditionally. It is a prerogative of the meek subjects to find glorification of their virtues through the unselfish sacrifice indispensable in order to enter the circle of people subjugated to the will of my Master. This is what we are, that is the true meaning of the word *slave*, and the sooner the world accepts our condition, the greatest our reward will be. The adepts are growing in number as well as increasing their devotion, ready to sacrifice themselves for the most perfect man who ever graced the earth. One of them will be spared to become a queen, no longer a servant but a mistress, a woman who will feed on his beauty and experience the nirvana, each and every day of her life. I would do the impossible to be that woman, but my days are numbered and I have already become too enervated to escape my final destiny. The question is: who will strike the crucial blow? The answer might never be found . . . But then again, I do not really wish to know.

CHAPTER 17
Le Rayon Vert (part 1)

The green ray or green flash. In French: *le rayon vert*. Why am I writing about this rare optic phenomenon? There is a simple element connecting me to Seven: the illusion. I am entitled to it right now; I am living on nothing, without any expectations at all, thus completely stripped of my capacity for hope. All I have got is my love for Seven and its mystical embodiment, which is merely an illusion, albeit a very persistent one. It is so painful to know I can read into him so deeply, yet have no means to reach that far into his life. I am praying for the magic of the brief single moment similar to a green flash, to bring me close to Seven's heart. Is it possible? What question is this that cannot be answered by the author of the illusion itself? The painful decline of an entire existence, goes on public display (I have told you I was a masochist, so do not pretend to be surprised) for everybody's consumption. The cannibals hungry for human flesh, have no respect for the sacredness of life, even my own.

Let us wait patiently, facing the same ocean he is facing, on a solitary afternoon with clear sky and calm waters. He would walk lost in his thoughts, the demon confined to a place light years away from where he is. He would stop and take a moment to breathe in the salty air, his lungs inundated with oxygen, his mind alert and solid. The concrete under his feet does not feel too hot; the sun is shining brightly, sending rays of compassion down to the earth, moist and willing to accept a new gift from nature. The boy salutes the seagulls hypnotised by the call of the sea; his face is glowing with happiness, but his heart is searching for answers to questions too frightening to be asked. Before him, the horizon symbolically embracing his future quest, the magician ready to play another trick on his young, ever changing conscience. But Seven cannot be nine again, he cannot even be sure there was a time when he was nine. He finally sits on the quay to contemplate, thinking back over his lost childhood days. He was loved and cherished, and when menacing forces were lurking in the shadow, he felt protected. He never quarrelled with anyone, only complied with every one's wishes, and whenever he looked bemused or lost, his mother would appear to take him home, the safe haven where he always belonged.

At times he felt almost invincible, unaware of the miry road ahead; it did not matter, a 9-year-old boy believes in something as eternal as age-old trees (but they also die, do they not?). He was thrown into the hustle and bustle of city life, but there was still plenty of room in his heart, he had not made any wrong choices yet. It takes some stupidity to ignore the opportunities presenting themselves, the fretful ego perhaps confused by the many filibusters preoccupied with their spoils. The egocentric man is no underachiever, contrary to common belief. The awareness of what needs to be accomplished is strong, the more so when the same words are spoken over and over, words that do not reflect true thoughts or feelings. They are wrongly convinced they can explain and give a name to the chaos building up in his head, but that is very likely a job for a psychotherapist. The boy is desperately searching for self-belief and self-confidence, whilst they are overwhelmed by the cynical criticism which confines them to play second lead in what appears to be a messy affair. When the feral cats hanging around his childhood home backyard needed to sort things out, they always got into a fight, tussled and went off chasing each other, and he could never tell if victory over an arch enemy invading one's territory, was as sweet as the knowledge that peace would last only if a fence was put up to keep the hostile forces away.

He built up his own fence and kept everybody out of his domain, occasionally allowing Mother and Father in, but not for too long. He did not want to give the impression he was lowering his guard, a sign of weakness he could not bear either in himself or in anyone else, for that matter.

He was never weak, only more sensitive than children his own age: he somatised. His talent was never in doubt, but the nature of the man could not escape being over-analysed. The poignant sweetness of his soul was questioned and mocked, leaving scars to remind him always not to trust anyone but his own instinct.

Nothing has truly changed. Here, facing the ocean and pondering over things to come, this man discovers the green spot above the sun, a bright green flash melting in his eyes of the same colour. The law of propinquity works like a charm for the chosen one; he develops a profound bond with the essence of life, which comes from water, and therefore finds himself inebriated by the awareness of the physical and psychological proximity to it. His body temperature rises, the excitement is tangible: he longs to be seen, heard, idolised.

You see, a life (any life) is unique, no mould is identical to the other, but his arrival generated turmoil and insanity, as well as adoration and joy. Quite to be expected when dealing with a rare example of a godlike creature, shaped into a sportsman (as lithe as a panther) gifted with unprecedented talent, and a man (as balanced as an upturned pyramid) plagued by inconsistency. Carl Jung would have studied his innate duality and analysed the interplay of opposites, creating the conflict and the attraction. Pity that Jung has been dead since 1961!

A considerable number of thinkers and intellectuals have written about the human condition. It is the condition of the entire human race, cursed by the same common destiny from the very moment life begins. The condition in which we find ourselves but we constantly try to avoid, looking for distractions resulting in the kind of fulfilment only meant to last for a limited time; it is that very thing pushing us to prove ourselves, inspiring us to excel and succeed, often against all odds. For some of us this is hardly bearable, while for others it is nothing but a glitch. Seven belongs to the latter. I do not count, for I cannot change my intimate nature. But he can and he does, as long as he continues ignoring the warning signs of his own illness, which I can clearly detect and–I am sure–so can others (though they would never have the guts to speak about it, afraid they would lose his love and attention). I, on the other hand, have nothing to lose, so I can endlessly hold forth on it.

The human condition, we said. Apparently, the complexity of our structure elevates us above other species. They do not call it the *animal condition* after all. But what if, just like the green ray on the horizon, our entire existence was only a flash of light in the immensity of an obscure dimension, randomly chosen by a mathematical equation? What if . . . I was that glitch in Seven's hidden darkness? Beauty is only skin deep, take the layer off and you can see how ugly the flesh will look. The involucre is as fake as a faithful man; it lies and deceives just like everything else that is human. Expect not to find resolutions in chaos: it is all purely accidental.

He gazes upon the horizon in amazement and awe, like the 9-year-old boy he once was; he sees the light, saves the moment in his memory and then, as he lifts his head up to the sky, he gets wind of something: a scent maybe? A voice? Or is it a song? A woman? A gorgon? Perhaps a stranger. Right up there . . . Yes, he knows there is something or someone who is reading his thoughts and spreading words about him, words he cannot even fully comprehend. At first, he does not know what to make of it, but then he has a vision, almost like an apparition. Although he has never encountered this figure before, he is not afraid. Maybe it is a celestial being, or just a trick of the mind. Whatever that might be, an irrepressible desire to grab it gradually pervades him. But he cannot catch something so volatile and ethereal which slips away softly, vanishing in the same imperceptible way it has appeared. It leaves behind an aura of sanctity and peace, a vision to reflect upon, as the sun is setting and the air becomes cooler, refreshed by a soft ocean breeze. He does not feel cold, there is warmth in his body, accustomed to shiver for quite a variety of other reasons. His body . . . Too much has been written already, and yet it is not enough. Will it ever be enough, I wonder? As insatiable and sinful as it is, the body of a man is also his holy land. The human condition makes it so: inviolable and unassailable (on paper, at least). His body awaits to be savaged, and we cannot avoid resembling those flesh-eating zombies wanting a piece of it for our own survival; we aspire to become gourmet chefs, specialised in the accurate preparation of a succulent, delicious dish, then feasting upon the remains like a bunch of vultures, because this is what we really are, in the end. The voracity of our souls devouring a helpless body, is a sight too gruesome to tolerate, even though the world has witnessed this kind of orgies for a very long time. The innocent boy is no longer there, not in the same form as it used to be; the man inside–the pulsating, hot-blooded, risk-taking man–has taken over the operations, the phylogeny of this specimen fully reckoned.

The peace residing in his kind heart, its naïvety in contrast with the ruthlessness of his actions; all the elements providing structure to a vagrant existence, the emotional journey to stardom, the sense of emptiness slightly touching him on rainy days, the doubts hovering on the edge of his mind, the vainglorious world he belongs too, its certainties and contradictions. Is there anything more to add to Seven's apotheosis?

I have seen the dark shadows, felt their cold embrace, but still I glorify this beautiful creature, who is totally unaware of what it means to be completely possessed, utterly insane, in love with everything that he is, as well as what he should never be. He does not have to witness all the ugliness in the world, we must keep a vigil eye on him, so that he will be spared the evil of their ways. They, the ones who have no creed, are blasphemous fiends, ferocious beasts, hellish freaks like Harpies,[1] and he must not be snared by them. He never will, I am sure. François and Marie are his devoted guardians, the father who owes his fortune to the miraculous son, and the mother, angelic and virtuous like Raffaello's Madonna d'Orléans. He trusts his life to them and they repay the trust with incomparable zeal, never missing an opportunity to rejoice at his success and glorify his exploits: the perfect parents to an unblemished son.

A collective psychosis takes hold of this modern time of ours, sparing no one, not even the sumptuous green-eyed man. Feeling crippled by anxiety, he develops a phobic fear and avoidance of certain situations, but he has got the rest of his life to sort himself out, surviving all the challenges, sailing through stormy seas to reach a final destination. It would be far more than what the rest of us could accomplish. As usual, there will be something showing the way, the light in his soul will stir him away from self-blame and regret. An intimate moment this is, where he can ponder over things that have been, and those yet to come. The refraction of light in the atmosphere causes the intense flash of emerald green, enhanced by a mirage lasting for a few seconds; his life will go as quickly as that, but filled with the same magic, nonetheless.

A thunderbolt fallen out of a clear sky, suddenly turns his face into a pensive frown. The calm before the storm: he reflects on this expression and agrees with it. Rain clouds gather, in the air pervaded by an electrical charge and the distinctive ozone smell. It rains on his perfect moment now forever gone; it wets his skin, cold shivers spreading all over his body, making him curse aloud.

'Putain de pluie! Il pleut à verse: ça craint!'2

A little dog approaches him out of nowhere, shaking off the rain which is pouring down copiously.

'Et toi, mon petit chien?'3

The dog barks at him twice, then shakes some more rain off. Imitating the same action, Seven shakes droplets of water off his head, his hair is so wet and the skin on his body visibly wrinkled. The sound of roaring thunder fills the air; right above the horizon Lei Kung, Thor and Ninhar4 are sending down dimly glowing bolts that meet with sparks, creating majestic lightning strokes. He is cold, but does not seem to mind it, enchanted as he is by the natural beauty of the phenomenon he is witnessing. The dog is now barking insistently, sounding worried and anxious; it is a black French Bulldog, an adorable creature who is trying to grab Seven's attention in every possible way. He reluctantly follows the dog, and just a handful of seconds later, a lightning strike hits the very spot he was standing before.

'Tu m'as sauvé la vie, mon petit chien. Merci!'5 The heartfelt thank you is acknowledged by the small canine with a polite wag of the tail.

Once they have completed their task, the three thunder gods quietly disappear into the falling darkness. Night time is fast approaching, as the last light of day quickly fades away.

'Quel est ton nom, mon petit chien?'6 The dog has no collar, but is quite friendly and obviously smitten with Seven. Out of the blue, a foghorn can be heard, piercing the air with a deep sound distracting them both for a short moment; Seven scans the horizon for signs of a ship, but can only conclude that either his eyes are deceiving him, or there is an invisible vessel out at sea. When he finally redirects his attention to his little friend, he is no longer there. To his amazement, he meets the eyes of a different creature.

'*Et vous? Qu'est-ce que vous faites ici?*'[7]

His question asked with much excitement and eagerness. It is now the calm after the storm, but it is cold and he has goose pimples. The touch of a soft hand brings warmth to his entire body, and a smile as bright as the sun in June, appears on his divine lips.

'*Merci!*'[8]

He speaks with a voice that could be barely heard. In a twinkling of an eye the green ray comes to life again . . .

(To be continued . . .)

CHAPTER 18
Divination

All my life I have been habitually late for everything: school, work, social engagements. I like to consider myself a late bloomer, perhaps invoking this as a great pretext for indefinite procrastination. Wearing a wristwatch has not helped at all; it is a mere formality, as I cannot be bothered to be on time despite the stress caused by being an inveterate latecomer. This has also put a severe strain on my conscience, a direct consequence of the good old sense of guilt (undoubtedly, a remainder of the infamous Catholic upbringing) insidiously seeding my mind with the kind of torment I cannot possibly rid myself of. For years, I did not even wear a watch, hence missing every single opportunity because my timing was naturally always bad. But blaming my misfortunes on not having a watch is just an excuse, as I can assure you that even with one, I keep having severe punctuality issues.

Certainly, it would have been so much easier if I had known in advance of future events, but that stuff only happens in movies. Well, it is not entirely true. In fact, some believers have access to a network of information that can make the art of divination possible. To a certain extent, they might also influence their own destiny to the point of making almost always impeccable choices. We call them *lucky people*, though luck has very little to do with it. Here comes Latin again, the language we all ought to study (it should be made compulsory): *'divinare'* ('to be inspired by a god.') Christians believe their god may enter into communication with them through dreams, and a few examples are indeed in the Bible, for instance in Numbers 12:6 ('He said, listen to my words: "When a prophet of the LORD is among you, I reveal myself to him in visions, I speak to him in dreams."')

More on the same line (also from the Bible) can be found in Job 33:14 sqq.: 'God speaketh once . . . By a dream in a vision by night, when deep sleep falleth upon men, and they are sleeping in their beds: then he openeth the ears of men, and teaching instructeth them in what they are to learn.'

Another fit definition for what we might call divination could be the 'intuitive perception' (which I am sure is something you all have plenty of), but it would be far more appropriate to describe it as 'the art or practice that seeks to foresee or foretell future events or discover hidden knowledge usually by the interpretation of omens or by the aid of supernatural powers.'

I am more inclined to accept the concept of inner knowledge gained through the interpretation of omens, especially the ones found in dreams.

As it happens, on the 6 March I had a very significant dream, one that left me in a state of bliss and kept me wondering about a number of possible meanings, in relation to my obsession with Seven. The dream had quite a lot to do with my handsome torturer, even though he did not physically appeared in it. Remarkably, once I woke up the first thought coming to my mind was: *I've just had the most beautiful dream ever!* I am not exaggerating, for that was the lasting impression it left on me.

François was the main protagonist in my oneiric vision. I got invited to his home by the beach, together with some other people we both seemed to know. Marie was not there, nor was Seven. The house was located on a small hill overlooking the sea, whose dark waters seemingly changed colours every time I glanced at them. Although they were agitated, they were giving out a clear sense of inner peace that is frankly impossible to put into words. It was a modern house, state of the art, I would say, especially the kitchen, which looked out on a pebble beach. I felt myself at home there, and asked if I could make some tea for every one present. François immediately agreed. The usually surly and detached François was being instead so nice and gentle. There were several photos of Seven as a child on the kitchen wall. I do not remember if we mentioned him at all. Perhaps we did, though it must have been just in passing.

Time transitions in dreams are weird, and this one was no exception. The next thing that happened involved us getting on a train which rode along the coast, unveiling a wild and breathtaking landscape. It must have been in the north of France, rather than the south. Do not ask me how I know this: I just do.

The dream ended with us collecting Marie from the station, then taking her back home. She was sweet and thanked me for looking after her husband, while she was away.

And right after that . . . I woke up.

The ocean, symbol of emotion and the subconscious mind, was a powerful sign in my dream. Jung interpreted it as a place of creativity, fertility and birth. But what was the ominous vision, the hidden message, the unspoken truth? If the train ride represented the smooth journey through life, then the overall interpretation of my dream will inevitably lead to some positive thinking. I am travelling down this road for a reason, this is not a waste of time, Seven did not appear into my life by accident. Even if our paths never cross, the man with green eyes and the woman without a place will have walked a distance together. This could be perceived as a peaceful outcome of a situation that so far has been painful and deceitful, but I have been scorned before and understand there is hardly ever an easy way out for me. The key words being illusion, deception, false hope: I have become acquainted with them, way back in the distant mists of time. There is nothing new here, only the same old aimless search, a treasure hunt without an X marking the spot, a blind race which takes me nowhere, because I do not even move an inch from my golden cage. Trapped in this empty existence, the longing for a merciful touch from my Master is none other than a flash in the pan.

Dreams are merely dreams. When morning comes, the spiteful sun shines its filthy light on the dusty chambers of my despair, and flushes away every sign of the night dreams that my memory cannot retain.

Friday 13:

I had to read those Egyptian tarots. On a day like this (a

lucky day for me), I simply could not resist the temptation of trying some divination of my own. Before you say anything, I must confess I am not particularly good at it; I have no such gift, so I am seriously struggling to make some sense out of the cards laid out in front of me. They have spoken of something bright and positive, but I wonder if they had a lot more to do with Seven's future than my own.

I have just read a comment about him, made by one of the familiar slaves, saying he is a womaniser. Sometimes I am shocked at the plain stupidity these people manifest. It does not take a clairvoyant to see that Seven is made for love, created to give and take pleasure; it is what he does best, also what he needs to do, and that is why we are his slaves. He excels in matters of love, but wavers between his own insecurities and his professional abilities. Without a doubt, he would make a rather interesting and engaging psychiatry case study. Then again, some things are better left unexplained, some dark corners untouched. It is the beauty of this particular beast.

The future may be too far away for him to worry about. And it is not the physical distance I am referring to, but more the concept in itself. We all have a secret wish to know about it, to find out if there will be love, companionship, success; we are less inclined to be told of the mishaps and the failures, of course, because they are already included in our curricula (disasters are awarded free of charge, as we know). Only heart matters interest us. Will we be married and have children? Will we find the perfect match? There are no signs to be interpreted, this is the simplest thing to do; everybody gets at least one chance to peep through the shutters of their future, not caring about the illusion. Some people may even be willing to pay real money for a guided tour of their own little insignificant existence.

The types of divination are varied and numerous. We are all familiar with astrology, a method using the position of celestial bodies (the sun, moon, planets, and stars) to determine their influence on human affairs. Also very popular is cartomancy (fortune telling using cards such as the Tarot), something I have tried to use myself, although with uncertain results. I do not know a single thing about clairaudience ('clear hearing' of divinatory information), but it sounds far fetched to me; clairvoyance ('clear seeing' of divinatory information) has

134

had a widespread reach throughout human history; crystallomancy (divination through crystal gazing) sounds fascinating; dowsing or divining rods (methods of divination where a forked stick is used to locate water or precious minerals) reminds me of something a paranormalist[1] would be very good at; numerology (the numerical interpretation of numbers, dates, and the number value of letters) I have occasionally used, yet I do find it almost infallible; oculomancy (divination from a person's eye) I have never heard of before, but it intrigues me a lot, especially when I think of predicting the future by looking into Seven's beautiful green eyes. Palmistry (the broad field of divination and interpretation of the lines and structure of the hand) is a very popular one and some years ago, I let a boyfriend of mine read the palm of my hand, and he predicted I would get married once (which I never did), so it turned out to be a load of rubbish, in the end.

To a certain extent, I do believe in precognition (an inner knowledge or sense of future events). Take me, for instance, I can often sense what is going to happen, though I can never act upon it. Somehow, I still cannot master this knowledge, so I have come to believe it is just another curse. I wish I was numb and did not feel a thing; instead, I see terrible events unfolding before my very eyes and cannot do anything to stop them.

Psychometry (the faculty of gaining impressions from a physical object and its history) could be possible, I guess; sciomancy (divination using a spirit guide, a method generally employed by channelers, also known as spiritualists) seems like hocus-pocus to me. Scrying (a general term for divination using a crystal, mirrors, bowls of water, ink, or flames to induce visions) is also something new to my ear, and it seems to include a lot of stuff which I am not particularly willing to investigate. I should definitely try tasseography (the reading of tea leaves remaining in a tea cup once the beverage has been drunk), since I am an avid tea drinker and would have plenty of leaves to examine (if only I knew how).

Some uncommon types of divination are worth a quick mention, starting from the one called omphalomancy, which involves counting the number of knots in the umbilical cord to predict how many more children the mother will have.

Then, there is the rather hilarious geloscopy, a form of

divination from the tone of someone's laughter. Two rather original types are also cromniomancy, a divination using onion sprouts, and the almost unpronounceable molybdomancy, drawing mystic inferences from the hissing of molten lead. One cannot leave out the yummy critomancy, the study of barley cakes (I am guessing I would be quite good at it). And last but not least, my favourite one: tiromancy, or divination by cheese! The choice is immense and bound to give you a headache: divination is by all means no laughing matter (or maybe it is, but that is entirely up to you)!

The conclusion to be drawn is that modern people are indeed very similar to their ancestors, deeply concerned with their future at the expense of their present, therefore constantly seeking reassurance, accepting that a perfect stranger would tell them what they should already know. It feels so much better when someone else confirms what we are subconsciously aware of; it could be a psychoanalyst or a fortune teller, it does not matter, as long as we hear it from another person's mouth. Why are we so afraid of introspection? The atavistic sense of incapacity to live up to our higher values, the fear of our own demise, the need to discover beyond the biological life a way to make amends: this is what could possibly be seen as the mainspring of all human actions.

My dream left a lingering sense of joy that lasted longer than expected. Yet, I cannot give real meaning or sense to something so inane, so immaterial. I remain steadfast in my criticism of the human nature, my scepticism reinforced daily by what I see and experience. At night I dream, I get a glimpse of an improbable future and cannot decide if it is my imagination at work, or simply a natural phenomenon too complex to be fully explained.

The ugly truth is that I know exactly where I am going; I am on that train with a one-way ticket, but I will not be coming back, because my destination is final. Unless, without a warning, the train I am riding on derails . . .

CHAPTER 19
Denial, Anger, Bargaining, Depression, Acceptance

What are prisoners on death row thinking, as their time to die approaches? What is the terminally ill patient sensing, during the final stages of his/her life? I have no idea; I only know that in my head there are thoughts that can be associated to the ones belonging to people who are certain about the moment of their own death. In fact, I find the similarities quite striking.

I am possessed by Seven's demon, and am experiencing a roller coaster of emotions only a mentally deranged person would go through; in most cases, these alternate states of consciousness do not even manifest themselves at all, yet in mine they are immediately recognisable. What follows, shall give you an accurate picture of the level of sickness I have now reached. [Feel free to openly comment on the subject. I am quite ready to be slammed.]

Denial.
I am not sick. I have fallen from grace, it is true, but it is only a temporary condition. He is a distraction, nothing serious. What do you say? Do I spend my days lusting over him and my nights fighting his demonic spirit? So, what if I do? There is nothing odd about it. I mean, yes I am detached from reality and often opt to ignore the signs of madness, but who does not have a little quirk or two? My condition is treatable, and I can be cured if I choose to. There is nothing excessive about my state of mind, and I am not going insane; in fact, every day I push to go

through the motions, therefore I am inclined to conclude that I can still perfectly function. Even though the mental debilitation is swiftly reaching the pain threshold, my spirit is in fighting form.

No, I am not sick. I am only obsessed. Deeply obsessed. Terminally possessed. (Is there some kind of consonance?) My anguish is the same as it used to be, only delusion has increased. I could not elaborate any further on my situation, I am sane (very sane): how could anybody deny it? Is there one person among you who would dare to call me sick? I am bursting with health, that is plain to see. I am perfectly fine, so fine I could almost die . . .

Anger.

What a bloody selfish, cruel, conceited young man! I have been knocking on his door, leaving messages, asking for a little attention, and what did I get in return? You guessed right: a big fat nothing!

Seven is selfish. He thinks exclusively of himself, concerned with his personal satisfaction and nothing else, occasionally giving hope only to a restricted maniple of faithful soldiers, whom he reckons will be worth his effort. He has placed his ego at the centre of my universe made of pain, suffering and blood spilt, and he is adamant to keep it there, at all costs.

The insignificant young whores he devotes himself to, are the sparkle animating his otherwise dull, yet consolidated routine. That is why no real progress is bound to take place. They could never make a man out of him, but are naturally easy to manipulate and control. At least he is clever enough to immediately recognise them, and consequently separate them from the likes of me. Actually, just from me. I must have a terrifying effect on him, because it is quite obvious that I scare him to death, and this is something that angers me beyond reason. It also makes me reflect on his stupidity: this damn boy can be so shallow, so childish. He is nothing like Monsieur Gilles–who has politely acknowledged my presence, and generously allowed me into a tiny waiting room inside his castle–or even like some of the other blokes belonging to Seven's trade, who are kind enough to keep the door ajar while they are away on their mission. I was wrong, he is nothing like them: he is worse, far worse! He talks

138

to Gilles's wife, showing kindness and consideration, but it is all an act. He could not care less about her, his heart overflowed with hypocrisy. I am disgusted at his cunning and audacity. Furthermore, he is cruel and spiteful, a professional attention seeker claiming to be in control, when in reality he has none, not even over his own bloody life.

He appears to have a very high opinion of himself, perhaps too high for his own good. He is so deluded! I do not need this modern day Narcissus[1] nor his inflated ego in my life: they can both go to hell, for all I care. The memory of Echo[2] will make me spurn the hideous man cravenly ignoring me.

Bargaining.

There will be room for one last attempt at gaining his trust, supposing that I could crush his resistance. Perhaps I could offer him a deal of some sort, a Faustian contract to allure him and make him reconsider his position in our little game of cat and mouse. Perhaps there will be no need to impose terms and conditions in order to fulfil the deal, a handshake will suffice. When all my offers are rejected, leaving me tearful and empty-handed, the only thing left to bargain away will be my dignity, sold at an affordable price to the monster with green eyes and that French *je ne sais quoi*.[3] Mephistopheles I cannot outwit, I try to understand life but fail to learn the language it speaks. 'All theory, dear friend, is gray, but the golden tree of life springs ever green.'[4] Then how come that I can only walk through the dark valleys, incessantly suffering the fire and brimstone of a sun glowing with white-hot flames? I wish my final offer would not be refused; still, I cannot break the rules in order to make things work. Nothing will ever change, no matter how many more times the moon will circle around the earth and the earth around the sun. 'In the end, you are exactly what you are. Put on a wig with a million curls, put the highest heeled boots on your feet, yet you remain in the end just what you are.'[5]

Depression.

Injuries, injuries and more injuries! Is he really this fragile?

At present time, what deeply concerns Seven is the immediate outcome of his career. He worries he might get some kind of injury that could end it prematurely, and who could blame him for feeling so insecure? I worry too, but I know whatever may happen, he will find a way to pursue his goals and finally make his mark. He is wrongly convinced that what he does is the only thing he has a real talent for, simply because he was told so; they made him believe that he could only excel in sports, since his mind was not ripe for anything else. It is unfortunate to have parents who encourage you only toward one direction, when there are hundreds of possibilities to express yourself fully. Had I been there, I would have told him to open his eyes and embrace a different kind of world: I have always had an immense belief in his gift.

This week, my mind is in the Middle East. There is so much of Seven lately, I am completely overdosing. Two entire days were spent feeding the addiction, still I am longing for more. I have an engagement I wish I could cancel, as it may interfere with the obsession. Usually, I do not allow anything to swerve me away from it, but I might be unable to avoid it this time.

He is becoming incredibly more handsome; indeed, the aura of destruction is finally visible to those who know nothing about his demonic side. So much beauty can surely kill you, and he is dangerously getting more aware of himself and his own might than he ever was before. Last year, when I encountered his demon, he was nothing like the man he is now, he was still a boy with flaws and insecurities. Nowadays, those very flaws have become his strength, turning into a form of power we are forced to reckon with, sooner or later.

The end is getting nearer, it is quite palpable now. Only a miracle could save me, yet I wish not to be spared, because my sickness is deeply rooted and shamelessly pleasurable.

Acceptance.
The irreprehensible horde of minions faithfully serving Seven, have come out in mass. I have no means to keep them at bay: I have been simply outnumbered. The gossip has become worse, with alleged romance, secret encounters and rumours of this or that affair, never confirmed nor denied by the parties involved. It feels like living in a virtual Babylon, belonging to a transient world of images and numbers; it is a tiresome activity

to keep up with the fast pace of the information highway, I struggle constantly and fall behind, because every one is faster than I am. I resign to my destiny, openly giving myself to the feisty demon who has captured the very essence of my soul. Resignation to one's fate is a tale as old as the world itself, it constitutes the biggest part of our existence; once we are overtaken by the young minds who engulf notions and technology, there is no bullet train we could catch to make up for lost ground.

I give up. I let them win. What could an obsolete intellectual offer to avoid going off the straight and narrow? They are young, resourceful and highly adaptable. I am yesterday's news, Seven might be looking at me like one looks at a curious piece in a museum, maybe an old coffee grinder that has no use or value nowadays, but is still nice to look at, perhaps generating some amusement at the evident rudimentary way of living of people from a previous generation. A joke, an outdated, rusted-out contraption: that is how he would see me.

Despite this fatal blow, I am standing tall, my heart still full of love. Someone once said: it is better to have loved and lost than never to have loved at all. I am not convinced this old adage is actually true, still pretty accurate nonetheless. Have I loved and lost? Maybe . . . But they are also losers, no use in parading their conquests. Accepting the ultimate defeat is the inevitable solution.

The above five stages might have raised more than an eyebrow amongst the few readers left at this point of the journey. The impact Seven has had on my life is far greater than this, and my account is only an infinitesimal part of the actual big picture. Days are numbered; there is always an end in sight, more or less visible even from a big distance. My curse and blessing at the same time, is to have that feeling heart, the pulsating organ digesting the emotions until I am enslaved by them.

Seven will never know real sadness, because he has a safe shelter to run to, some place where his demon is also allowed to stay. The same demon who is his own Svengali,[6] controlling every action, every beat of his heart. It is way too premature for Seven to sight the finishing line, or even perceive there is one awaiting his passage, but this is only due to logic; there is a time and a place to deal with sensitive topics, the time is still too uncertain and blurry, the place even more unfathomable. The slaves themselves do not bother with these types of arguments: I guess this is exclusively my prerogative. I am too ill to escape this subject, too close to the end not to discourse upon it.

The mere mention of the word death gives Seven a start; he was not born to die, my Master, as he not only came to gift us with life and enjoyment, but was also made to entertain us. There was no legal evaluation of the concept of demise in his contract, certainly no resolutory clause was included either, and although the terms were never fully discussed, it was implied the boy existed from the very beginning to enhance and underline beauty, happiness and sex (in no particular order). Seven understood right from the start that the negative would be swept under the carpet for him by the occasional minion on duty: he would have not signed the contract otherwise. Though someone will have to break the news to him, he cannot pretend to exclude such a significant part of the universal law from the agreement. Naturally, the choice will fall on his loved ones, who will have to explain the paradigm to him, and I imagine he will be laughing at them, so self-assured he is about his own immortality.

The singularity of Seven exceeds all limits, therefore it would be impossible to contain it and turn it into something more . . . manageable. In accepting the conditions of his unquestionable perfection, we waive our right to be heard, we become as silent as the grave, never to speak a word again. I am the rebellious slave, I have broken my promise and introduced you to the obsession; at the beginning, it must have been odd to read about it, although now it has become so familiar, you probably think everybody should get one. If only it was that simple!

Some of the unanswered questions are stumbling blocks, but perhaps it is better this way. I believe that mystery constitutes a considerable part of Seven's charm, the dogmatic acceptance of his essence is the *conditio sine qua non*[7] of our slavery, which seems to be constantly evolving, transforming itself from the harmless infatuation of the early days into a more permanently diseased state of mind. The hereditary taint plays a part in this evolution, and those of us who are marked with it will never truly free themselves.

Death row prisoners, terminally ill patients, animals in slaughterhouses, myself, my peers, the dying swan: what is our common cosmic fate? We fight against the gravitational pull of the black hole, hoping not to be sucked into the void. Sooner rather than later we die, some of us peacefully, others with bitter regret. The innocent ones, instead, will fall without even knowing why; their eyes, where purity resides, manifesting the inconfutable signs of terror, their piercing cry for help pervading the air, unheard in the solemn indifference of an empty planet.

CHAPTER 20
Le Rayon Vert (part 2)

'*P*as de quoi, mon chéri.'[1] Minerve's radiant smile accompanies these five words, sustaining them for a long while. How could this be possible? How could she be here?

The place is where the green ray peeps in, emerging from sunrise with a new friend: the nearest star to the Sun, the one they call Proxima Centauri.[2] The solitary red dwarf star has found a companion, another planet orbiting at close range, redrawing the stellar course that brings together Seven and Minerve for one last time. Reunited again, joined in holy union beyond the horizon, as a new day is dawning and the infinite power of the sun is showing mercy on all things mortal.

Seven is the Sun, Minerve Proxima Centauri; you can see their shape, colour, substance, you can almost touch them if you try hard enough. Meant to be together, to defy the boundaries of time and space, existing as the exact opposite, as the magnetic force that resurfaces from the dark obscurity of pain. They are an image of beauty, love and devotion. Witness their magnificent splendour, kneel before their might; like Aztec gods they stand taller than the pyramid of the Sun, appearing majestic to the eyes of their subjects. A sight to be treasured and remembered for many more centuries to come.

The light in Seven's eyes makes them appear so much brighter, that Minerve has to turn away from his dazzling stare. It is a blinding light, the kind one sees when staring directly at the sun.

The two lovers are finally here, facing the ocean, because in this universe their story comes full circle. I will be Minerve for one last performance, while Seven will be showing his real face for the very first time.

The girl I once was did not differ a great deal from the boy with green eyes; I too loved climbing up the trees, curiously wondering how long they had been on earth and who planted them. Yes, perhaps they die some day, killed by a human hand or just consumed by old age, but I know of a Great Basin Bristlecone Pine *(Pinus longæva)* called Methuselah, germinated in 2832 BC and still alive to this very day. The long-lived tree is 4,841 years old! I have never been to the White Mountains of California to visit this pine, though one day I would love to go there with Seven. Unsurprisingly, he was not acquainted with the existence of Methuselah until I told him all about it. It is implied there is plenty more that I could teach him, but what could I learn from him? The child is going to show me the face of flawless beauty, guiding me through the events of the past that forged his spirit and shaped his temperament, for once leading me towards a final victory to share with him only. It does not matter that he is nine and I am twenty-eight.

Seven and Minerve are just beginning to make plans for their future. A huge chunk of time is erased so quickly, almost wiping out at once the fundamental laws of physics. But you (like the two of us) have to use your imagination as well, and project yourselves into this pseudo-reality, where anything you wish is possible, even the sheer impossible. Here we are free, eternal, moving from one age to the other, defying space and time yet again.

It is the summer of 1995, and South Africa wins the Rugby World Cup over New Zealand at Ellis Park in Johannesburg, with Nelson Mandela presenting the trophy to the South African captain Pienaar. France finish third in the competition, much to Seven's delight.

Minerve is boarding a train that will take her back to Paris. Every year, she spends two whole months in Nîmes, the capital of the Gard department, perfecting her French while also attending a visual arts workshop in the Languedoc region. Then she flies back to the States from Paris. She has just turned twenty-eight, but the thought of pushing thirties does not faze her. Life has been often generous with Minerve, giving her almost everything she desired, yet she has never stopped searching for new ways to express her talent and passion.

Her train will reach the *gare de Lyon*[3] in four hours. The long ride excites her every time; she observes the other passengers with the inquisitive eyes of a child, making up stories in her mind, imagining pieces of their lives before and after the journey. But two travelling companions catch her eye more than the others. A father and his son enter the train compartment, the young boy slightly smiling at her, while his dad stashes their two suitcases in the luggage rack above the seats. The boy gets to seat by the window, facing Minerve who is reading *The Sorrows of Young Werther* by Johann Wolfgang von Goethe (the French edition called *Souffrances du jeune Werther*). As she raises her head to say *bonjour,*[4] the train slowly starts leaving the station. The kid's father nods, then takes his seat next to the boy. Before going back to her reading, she glances at the child one last time: the green ray shines in his eyes. *This is going to be a perfect journey*, she thinks to herself, right after a whistle is heard from far away, and Father and Son engage in discussion over their own dreams and expectations. They talk so fast, their chattering cannot be understood by her; she can only grasps they are heading for Paris, where something very exciting must be in store for both members of this little family. She hopes to have a man and a son like them, some day; everything is possible at this point in her life, most of all love and motherhood. If only she could unlock the future and decipher its ramifications to the present. That is all she is looking for, all that she needs. Something real to believe in, before falling into the clutches of time and never dream of happiness again.

The train reaches Clermont-Ferrand,[5] some of the passengers are getting off, as new ones board it. Minerve is collecting her thoughts; she will be finishing the book by the time the pillars of the *gare de Lyon* are in sight. Werther commits suicide at the end of the tale by Goethe, because he cannot have the love of Charlotte: what is the use of living a life devoid of love? Without the cynicism of later years, she can answer the question in the twinkling of an eye. Life is worth nothing if you forget to love. Better take the conium, the toxic poison hemlock, and leave peacefully before some more damage is done to a life already deprived of its marrow. Werther shoots himself, it is an ordinary death, a pitiful one, nonetheless. Liberty at all costs, freedom from the chains of existence and the ineluctability of fate. The core of human nature immutable, no matter how many centuries separate us from our ancestors. Ironic, is it not?

Seven is only a boy, unaware of what lies ahead; he trusts his father, relies on the few certainties a 9-year-old boy might have, but cannot foresee the events that are going to change his history, transforming him into a demonic creature, forever bound to the earthly charade. As for Minerve, she is going to break so many times that recollecting all the pieces will be almost impossible; some will never be recovered, so she will have to do without a few parts of her shattered heart. But there will be no resignation in her, only bitter torment, which is by far more than enough, my friends. Still, when finally reunited with her handsome demon, she will be happy. At last, a semblance of reason left to mark her passage on earth, dutifully handed down to posterity.

What do they have in common, these chosen players in the comedy of errors we witness every single day? Perhaps they are terrified by the obscure meaning of their own journey; each singular motion propels their anguish a step further away from the beginning, when they were young and full of hopes. The longer the step, the more terrifying the approach; inevitably, they are seeking shelter after spreading heresy through their unholy behaviour, though they could not avoid being anathematised. But fear is a necessary ingredient; it is a primordial human instinct that secures survival, and our species is affected by it from the moment of conception to the final hour. The brazen ringleader, who can thwart his opponents pretending to be fearless, is destined to fall the hardest, and just like centennial oak trees in a forest felled by electric chainsaws, his fall will be the loudest. Make no mistake: there is no way to curtail the influence of a primeval trait. It all happens fast and certainly not painlessly. The bullet train breaks through the barrier of sound, to arrive on time and on schedule, while in the meantime, with surgical precision, the puppet master has crossed another name off his infernal list. It would take only a thousandth of a second to destroy the human masterpiece which took millennia to complete, but who cares? Minerve does not. She dreams of her own contribution to the cause of humanity, unsure about the consequences of her future actions. Seven is even more unaware; he is only nine and knows nothing, he barely knows his own name. They are shaping him, rounding off his rough corners like they would do to an inanimate object. And he lets them manipulate his soul, allowing the systematic disfigurement of the pure angel that he is, so perfect and innocent. He does not have the knowledge or shrewdness to object to the malicious defacement they are perpetrating, but some day soon he will be strong enough to take his revenge in the most exhilarating, almost comic-book-like manner. His triumph is our defeat, but we fit the mould, hence our resignation to the inevitable. It is pure conjecture to expect a role-exchange to take place in later years, after all there is only one Master and countless–yet devoted–servants. We are bought and sold, but never with a light heart, the merchandise is in high demand and deserves to be carefully handled. No refund. No second chance. You pay, you buy. That is it. There is no secret formula. The end justifies the means . . . Such a simple conundrum.

The last page of the book is turned. In Paris, there is no room for other thoughts; the evening rush has overcome the lulling rhythm of the train, its wheels no longer rolling down the track. It has now come to a full stop, and the passengers are getting off in an orderly manner, which clashes with the adrenaline-charged world outside. Minerve has got time for a quick bite at *Le Train Bleu* (she is dying for the mouth-watering *fleurs de courgettes*[6] and for the traditional *crêpes Suzette*[7]), the restaurant situated in the hall of the *gare de Lyon*, and named after the famous luxury night express train. In truth, this means at least an hour and a half of sumptuous dining, admiring the dazzling belle époque décor (left unchanged since 1901), while enjoying a fabulous meal, washed down with some rich and opulent Château Margaux.[8]

So, the wayfaring travellers now go their separate ways. For young Seven (and his father) this is a new beginning; for Minerve just another leg of a journey that has already covered many miles. But their paths will cross again, as they are meant to rejoin the very same road that brought them together, renouncing the petty idiosyncrasy to commitment, while embracing the complete, mutual devotion they once considered unfeasible.

And the time has finally arrived for Seven and Minerve to be reunited. Just like two waves in the salty waters, they will be dancing in harmonic beauty with the Oceanids,[9] hugging and kissing, producing the sweetest music to hypnotise the sea mermaids, who once again have emerged from the deepest pits of the abyss. The Sun and Proxima Centauri become magnetised in the presence of the ocean, absorbing its living, pulsating energy. The unlikely lovers project their blinding light beyond the horizon, with a fierce beauty that has no boundaries, and they shall nevermore be afraid of what it will be. Seven must embrace his fate, always maintaining a defiant stance, no matter how many times he will be denied victory. This is the trait of a true champion, the essential quality of a real man. It will take him a very long time to learn this lesson, but there are role models to inspire him; one is the friend whose demeanour exudes humility, something he needs to work on himself, because a righteous man is humble above all things. The other is his mother, a woman of integrity and sound principles he should always honour and respect. The future has not been written yet, the solid hands of time are securing his safety on earth, but his invisible companion cannot provide the shelter he needs. He has to find it himself, alone in this quest, as no one could volunteer to carry the weight of the world in his place. If he succeeds, he would be only fulfilling his destiny, but should he fail, the chasms of hell will be opening under his feet, and he will be dragged all the way down to the centre of the earth, where there is no escape from the perpetual torture of a remorse of conscience.

'*Je dois disparaître*'[10] she says, disappear, go into the invisible state of oblivion, though not for long; twenty-four years in this universe last only the time of a quick sigh from the gods.

'*Non, tu ne dois pas disparaître, Minerve!*'[11] Seven weeps, unveiling his fear of never seeing her again, a sight that touches her heart once more.

'*Souviens-toi de moi, mon amour, quand tu me rencontreras . . . N'oublie jamais que je t'aime et surtout qu'il faut battre jusqu'au bout, il ne faut jamais jeter les armes.*'[12]

149

One last kiss to dry his tears, one ever lasting look into his green eyes, then she vanishes into thin air. Farewell to my beautiful boy, *adieu!* The ocean intones a funeral litany, the veil is drawn over this touching moment, never to be lifted again: *alea iacta est!* The die is cast, the celestial design brought to completion, our solemn promise shining like a precious emerald set in the green ray forever.

CHAPTER 21
The End?

My computer is overloaded with photos of Seven, and I am sure it is going to die on me, one of these days. Looking for evidence? Its illness is not just a passing fad, it gets worse every day; the bloody machine keeps sabotaging this diary, losing its pages, deleting words and sentences out of the blue. There is no mistake: this technological instrument is sending out clear signals of an imminent demise.

I have collected so much valuable information, I could write a book about Seven, this way becoming his unofficial biographer for the joy of all his other faithful slaves. But of course, I have no intention to write anything of the kind; my goal is to feed the addiction, keeping it alive and present, in spite of all the things that are indeed more important and significant in a woman's life.

As the latest (reoccurring) injury strikes again, Seven flies back home (wherever that is, these days), leaving us all high and dry. I have seen history repeating itself so many times before that I am now immune to the consequences. If there is any consolation, at least this sod's law does not spare anyone. I wonder if the real Seven ever thinks of his own demise; I would love to believe he does, that he is a little bit more like me, perhaps handling doubts and questions the way I do. The journey that started when he was only nine years old is meant to continue a lot longer than he knows, the conformity of our society will not change a thing, for everything has already been written in the stars. Unfortunately for those like me, this is an absolute truth that cannot be denied. We are the sum of the celestial equations resulting from the initial chaos; we never change and yet, we progress through time and space like meteorites on course to collide with asteroids.

April 3:

The fall from grace has forced Seven to retrieve in his home town in the south of France. There he goes, back to his roots and the safety of his birth home; he is so lucky to have a shelter like that when he needs it the most, when events take a bad turn, his health deteriorates and the only true solace is his mother, the divine Marie, who knows exactly how to make him feel better. Only mothers know that!

As for me, I am coping. Seeing that he is safe and in the care of his loved ones, gives me comfort and some peace of mind. It is all temporary; soon I will be facing my final moments, giving in to fear and sheer panic. I will be searching for my prince, only to find his demon, deprived of the essential part that makes Seven what he is: a soul. The soulless being will be wearing the headsman hood, hiding his face but showing the green rays of torture, relentlessly shining in this pitch black darkness. They will be the last light I see, before the axe is lowered to take this life away, to finish off this sad excuse for a woman, ending the pain of a tragic existence. It sounds almost poetic when in fact it is perverse and shallow. What will I do facing the handsome executioner, in the heat of my final moments? Will I be fighting? Will I be weeping? What would I say, if words were to be spoken?

Today I walked for hours, under the cold rain and wind, searching for shelter. I found it in a small church, I am not sure about the exact denomination, but a Christian one for certain. A cemetery surrounded it, and before I stepped inside, I caught a glimpse of a shadow walking briskly and then disappearing into the building. Although I wanted to enter, a sense of shame permeated through my body, so I did not move.

From the outside, the place appeared to be empty, when suddenly the music of an organ could be heard. But I still could not see anyone inside. I finally plucked up the courage and entered. In the bare ante-chamber there was only a table with some books and leaflets, a box for donations and two benches, each under a big window. There was also a book where people left their thoughts and signed their names. I did the same.

When I entered the middle door leading into the actual church, the music was still playing; someone was indeed rehearsing a succession of musical pieces, there was hardly a quiet moment, yet it did not bother me in the slightest. The acoustics of the church were flawless, I got almost mesmerised by the sound of the organ gently filling out the ambience. I sat down and waited for the storm to pass, but it did not. After a while, I returned to the ante-room and decided to sit on one of the benches. I stared at the window on the opposite side for a very long time. The music finally stopped and I could hear footsteps; the small middle door opened, revealing a pleasant young woman carrying what appeared to be some piano scores in her hands. She smiled, and I offered my apologies as though I was not supposed to be there at all. But she kindly invited me to sit inside, where it was warm. She did not know I had already sat in a pew in the middle of the west side of the nave, so I pretended I had just arrived. After she left, I went back inside and this time I sat in the silence of the church, with only the voice of the wind to keep me company. I started to weep as my thoughts converged on the one, ultimate conclusion: my fallible life must come to an end.

I left a small offer in the donation box, just to thank the church for the shelter it had given me during the stormy weather. Then, I quietly left.

Ironic how for a non-believer a place like that makes actually more sense than expected. But only because it was empty (except for the organist), no one could see or hear my torment: no one in the material world, that is.

A life is never demanded by its rightful owner, but it can always be taken away if truly unwanted. Seven would cling onto his own with all his might, fighting tooth and nail to keep it intact and safe. Even when he fails, the result is just a flesh wound for him, it heals in no time. He cares not for the damned ones, certainly not when he carries with him an aura of invincibility. And even though with just a snap of his fingers he could rescue them, he ultimately chooses not to.

Almost a year has gone, since I started this journal, and I

have gained nothing but pain from it. Hope I will manage to get to Seven's twenty-third birthday, though I am aware it will take a miracle. I might be tempted to sign out before that day, and you will be left alone, deprived of the historian supposedly able to report word for word the apotheosis of the young monster with green eyes. Then, you will be forced to rely on the other slaves and their sloppy reports. It will not be the same, they cannot be trusted and furthermore, their cannibalism is the appalling means to an end. There would be nothing left of Seven, nothing worth to die for, my dear friends. He will be eaten alive, devoured by the fiendish servants, with no one to fling back the poisonous breath of death.

Humans fear death. They often wonder about the afterlife: is there one? So far, no one has come back to tell us, therefore I will be more inclined to believe that when we die we just go back into oblivion, our body starts rotting away until soon after, it is reduced to a mere heap of bones. We are not able to remember where or what we were before conception, and certainly we will not have a feeling of where or what we will be after our biological death. Unless, there really was an afterlife. I personally would take the agnostics position that life after death cannot be verified, but I am also fascinated by the thought of eternal recurrence, as it appears in some of the works by Friedrich Nietzsche. He wrote as follows:

> 'What, if some day or night a demon were to steal after you into your loneliest loneliness and say to you: 'This life as you now live it and have lived it, you will have to live once more and innumerable times more' ... Would you not throw yourself down and gnash your teeth and curse the demon who spoke thus? Or have you once experienced a tremendous moment when you would have answered him: 'You are a god and never have I heard anything more divine.'
> [The Gay Science, 341]

In 1872, the French political activist Louis Auguste Blanqui also wrote about a theory of eternal return in his astronomical work entitled *L'Eternité par les astres*. It holds some kind of fascinating appeal, I suppose, to consider the universe as something recurring an infinite number of times; it is undeniably intriguing and morbidly enticing, but as all theories go, even this one will have only a placebo effect on the minds of sceptical humans such as myself.

But enough of this! I have not an ounce of hope left in me, so what do I care if I live or die? Perhaps tomorrow will bring me an answer: wishful thinking, my soul hates you.[1]

Today, the shocking news broke the icy silence in this life of mine, barely hanging on a thin thread and almost over and done with. Seven's demon has been let out, unleashed, freed from whatever chains were holding him down. He has completely taken over the mind and soul of my prince, single-handedly destroying the present and immediate future with an exceptional, unparalleled fury. He is out of control; no one seems to be able to stop this ferocious fiend, mercilessly putting an end to Seven's career. I knew that it would happen, I just did not expect the moment to be now; just as my own life becomes muddled with misery, Seven's world is shattered and he loses everything he has: his reputation, status, credibility. It is all gone, wiped out. Neither François nor Marie could really rescue him this time; they are finding it so hard to hold onto their pride without losing faith in the boy, rapidly turning into a man with a tarnished name. He has let them down, but how could they not hear his cry for help? He has been sending messages all along, requests gone unheard, and now the demon is out and there is nothing they could do to bring him back in. It is time for the scales to fall from their eyes, as this is no *Slovakian incident*, no little mischief: this is hell! The unrepentant demon takes advantage of the little child, the one we have seen struggling to emerge and whose lackadaisical attitude reflected his unhappiness, as well as the ever increasing inner sadness.

How could he be happy, if I am not there with him? How can I be happy, if he is not here with me? Haphazardly seeking his elusive self, Seven encounters more difficulties than he could ever bear to face; he is resigned, almost passive before the menacing demon who runs his life, controls his psyche and betrays his conscience at will. He is helpless, but more importantly, he is alone with the monster and scared to death to succumb in an unequal fight that has lead him to the point where his back is

against the wall, and he does not know where to turn. It is torture, he just wishes he could disappear, but of course he will not.
He stays, ready to face the scorn poured on him by his family; he
looks defiant, it is true, but inside his heart is breaking. The demon has scarred him with an unprecedented vengeance, turning
his gift into a cumbersome impediment; it must have been a distraction, or perhaps a word spoken too hastily and with the carelessness of youth, something of a delicate nature coming
abruptly between them, thus a power struggle ensued. Seven
was the one left standing with the unwanted loot, innocently trying to explain how this had been only a mistake, but the clever
demon, so easily knowing his ways into the young man's intricate mind, used his best tricks to finally push him into a corner,
sadistically revealing the Devil's dandruff as my Master's treacherous accomplice.

My boy framed by his own negligence disguised as a demonic pleasure. He could not have been more ready for crucifix-
ion than he realised, and consequently, in a surprising reversal
of roles, the saviour now needs to be saved by the humble servant he so generously came to rescue from the brink of death. I
could not have concocted anything more elaborate, not even if I
had wanted to. Life imitates art far better than art imitates life.
No flattery here, just the plain truth. Seven needs his slaves
more than they need him, and that, my friends, is something I
would call extraordinary. *Point barre.*[2]

Time is torture. Time spent like this is unbearable torture. I
must put an end to the charade. I know you would want to find
out about Seven's fate, but that could take months, even years,
and I cannot bear this anguish any longer. It is not the end of the
obsession, but rather its final transformation. Seven's troubles
will be resolved in the end, mine are on a more permanent scale.
I am nothing to him: an undisputed fact of primary importance.
O, woe is me!

The fall of the gods, with their heavy tumble on this earth
that could not stop spinning, is something marking every human
era, but perhaps the obscenity here lies in the mere carelessness
in which this (utterly unexpected and deeply blameworthy)
incident has occurred. So why do I have to pay even for his silly
mistake? I point my finger at all the players involved in this

pantomime; they are all to be blamed and despised, all equally responsible for the complete mess resulting from my Master's mischievous act.

This is it from me. I will be permanently closing this door, because writing is a curse that will eventually lead to suicide, and I am already half-dead, all that is needed is either a gun, a blade, a rope or perhaps some barbituric acid. How pathetic if this journal was to become my own testament! Or worse: the longest suicide note ever written. It is not what I had meant for it to be; my intention was to elevate and praise the glory of a man whom I had only dreamt of, never believing for one moment he could exist in real life. I meant to express my love and complete devotion the only way I knew, considering that I am not young, certainly not pretty; I had no options, I could not even become a stalker. Therefore, the sole means by which I could elaborate this overwhelming feeling, was through my (presumed) ability to write. I fell in love with Seven when he was battered, bruised and beaten, and now that my journey is over, I leave him in a similar predicament. I am fully aware that he would instinctively refuse the help of a stranger; furthermore, what could I have to offer that would ease his pain? Only more pain, my own, which is possibly leading to an untimely end.

Yes, I do love Seven with all my heart. I see his soul, I sense his despair and fear his fears; I laugh at his jokes, smile at his naïvety and in the end, I just resign myself to his beauty. Paraphrasing Arthur Rimbaud, I am 'sinking down into the most horrible blackness'.3 I am not sure I wish to go any further, even though my obsession is still very present, not to mention alive. I will be pushing up daisies before you are done reading this book.

My life has been milked to the last drop, my will to live it replaced by the will to end it. I do not know how, but I am free to choose when; however, what I cannot control is this urge to reach out to Seven and let him know that the joy caused by the mere acknowledgement of his existence has been much higher than the pain of not sharing it with him. I was wrong earlier when I said that he would never experience the kind of sorrow I have been so accustomed to, though I am quite sure he will manage to survive it more easily.

Suffering the painful martyrdom is the kind of test he

would gladly do without, and yet he goes through it with a stoical mind, infinite courage and spirit of endurance. I lack such qualities, and have no moral support to face the daily struggle. Weak is my mind and everything it produces. My final written words have not the audacity to be remembered, or the presumption to heal the sadness of living; they are the last ones I will write, for there shall be nothing else to say, once Seven has taken a leave of absence. And until his return, if ever there is going to be one, it all ends here, on the barbwire surrounding this prison I try to break out from, only to find myself stuck in a constant spiral, condemned to have feelings that rot inside this empty shell. The mortal coil survives, barbiturates in one hand, the picture of demonic beauty in the other.

I am on my way out to buy some whiskey, hoping that benzodiazepine[4] mixed with alcohol will eventually provoke an overdose. What do you know? They are out of flumazenil.[5] These freaking words refuse to jump out the page and finish me. I guess I will wait another hour, perhaps even another night. Seven is probably asleep now. He is my flumazenil. I had better stock up, should I change my mind tomorrow, and decide that I want to be saved.

Notes

1 The Beginning
[1] Reason for being, p. 2.
[2] My god! What a sight! P. 3.

4 The Obsession
[1] 'My darling, he feels disappointed.' P. 30.

5 The Real Seven
[1] Excerpt from *The Complete Poems of Henry Wadsworth Longfellow* (b.1807—d.1882), American poet, p. 38.

6 The Here and Now
[1] Literally 'god from the machine.' A person or event that provides a sudden and unexpected solution to a difficulty, p. 47.
[2] Literally 'a public or skilled worker.' A powerful creative force or personality, p. 47.
[3] My dear, 48.
[4] D.O.M. To the Lord, the best and greatest, p. 49.

7 Seven Holy Virtues, Seven Deadly Sins
[1] A misquote of *Credibile est, quia ineptum est* (It is to be believed because it is absurd), *De carne Christi 5.4* by Quintus Septimius Florens Tertullianus (b.150×160, d.220×240), a major theologian in the Christian Church, p. 50.
[2] The virile member, p. 54.
[3] In Greek mythology, the god of the sea and of earthquakes, p. 55.
[4] Quote from *The History of Juliette* (1797), p. 56.
[5] Donatien Alphonse François de Sade, Marquis de Sade (b.1740—d.1814), French nobleman and Novelist, p. 56.

8 The Disintegration of the Persistence of Memory
[1] France's national soccer team players and coach, p. 63.
[2] 'And the condom?' P. 65.
[3] 'Minerve . . . You make me hard. I want you.' P. 65.

9 The Sacred Profaned

[1] 'I can see that you're burning with desire.' P. 67.

[2] 'I get so incredibly hard.' P. 68.

[3] 'I want to lose myself in your mouth.' P. 68.

[4] 'I love to swallow your nectar so much.' P.68.

[5] 'You have a fabulous ass! I've never seen an ass like yours.' P. 68.

[6] 'What? Are you jealous?' P. 69.

[7] 'How many girls have given you a blow job?' P. 69.

[8] 'How many?' P. 69.

[9] 'You're the best!' P. 69.

[10] 'Come, take me again.' P. 69.

[11] 'I love shagging you. I love to see you come.' P. 69.

[12] 'Of course!' P. 69.

[13] 'Not at all!' P. 71.

[14] 'Come with me to the end of the world.' P. 71.

[15] 'Your body belongs to me, you belong to me . . .' P. 72.

[16] 'I love you!' P. 73.

[17] 'I love you too.' P. 73.

[18] Latin word for 'arrival.' Used for the Christian season of Advent, p. 73.

10 Voyeurs

[1] 'You're my bitch.' P. 76.

[2] 'You love my cock, bitch. You want me to hurt you? Come on, take this!' P. 79.

[3] 'I always want you . . . Like crazy!' P. 80.

11 Minerve

[1] 'Minerve: who are you really? Undress in front of me . . .' P. 81.

[2] 'Yes, please.' P. 82.

[3] 'Your bra, my beautiful . . .' P. 83.

[4] 'Play with your nipples. I want to see them harden . . .' P. 83.

[5] 'Take off your panties . . .' P. 84.

[6] 'You are naked. You are so beautiful, with your body never ceasing to tease me.' P. 84.

[7] 'My love.' P. 84.

[8] 'My beautiful . . . I want you so much.' P. 84.

[9] 'Speak if your words are stronger than the silence, otherwise keep silent.' P. 85.

[10] 'Carelessness? That's odd . . .' P.86.

[11] 'Loving is half of believing.' Victor Hugo, French poet and novelist (b.

1802—d.1885), p. 87.

12 The Father of My Child
[1] My beautiful, p. 92.

13 Nereida
[1] The Moldova in Czech is called Vltava. It is the longest river (440 km) in the Czech Republic, p. 99.
[2] Vladimir Samoylovich Horowitz was a Russian-American pianist (b.1903—d.1989). Widely considered one of the greatest pianists of the twentieth century, p. 99.

14 Erase and Rewind
[1] The amorous conversation:

SEVEN   Who do you want to be? Would you like to become my slave?

MINERVE   I pose no resistance. *Possessing me, thou shalt possess all things. | But thy life is mine, for God has so willed it. | Wish, and thy wishes shall be fulfilled; | But measure thy desires, according | To the life that is in thee. | This is thy life, | With each wish I must shrink | Even as thy own days. | Wilt thou have me?*

SEVEN   I'm delighted that we feel the same. You must understand that our love is eternal.

MINERVE   Are you ready to sacrifice your freedom for me?

SEVEN   You are my freedom, Minerve. You're the love of my life, my eyes dream only of you. Without you I am lost, and all alone I lose all hope.

MINERVE   My love . . . Love me as I love you. I know we need to be a bit similar, to understand each other, but also a little different in order to love one another.

SEVEN   I have no doubts . . . I'd love to be a daisy, so that you could pick my petals off, over and over, while speaking soft words to me.

MINERVE   The words of the poet . . . I will recite them for you, dear.

[*Honoré de Balzac, *La Peau de chagrin* (The Magic Skin or The Wild Ass's Skin) 1831] Pp. 103—4.

[2] Jacques Prévert, *Cet amour* (This Love) from *Paroles* (Words) © Éditions Gallimard; tr. Eliande Jacques (2010), pp. 104—6.

This love | So violent | So fragile | So tender| So desperate | This love | Beautiful like the day | And bad like the weather | When the weather is bad | This love so true | This love so beautiful | So happy | So joyful | And so ridiculous | Trembling with fear like a child in the dark | And so sure of itself | Like a quiet man in the middle of the night | This love that scared the others | That made them talk | That made them turn pale | This love watched for | Because we watched for it | Tracked down, wounded, trampled on, fulfilled, denied, forgotten | Because we tracked it down, wounded, trampled on, fulfilled, denied, forgot it | This entire love | Still so alive | And all sunny | It is yours | It is mine | That which was | This thing always new | And that has not changed | As real as a plant | As quivering as a bird | As hot and as alive as the summer | We can both | Go and return | We can forget | And then go back to sleep | Wake up | Suffer and age | Fall asleep again | Dream of death | Wake up | Smile and laugh | And rejuvenate | Our love remains there | Stubborn like a mule | Alive like the desire | Cruel like the memory | Stupid like the regrets | Tender like the recollection | Cold like marble | Beautiful like the day | Fragile like a child | It looks at us while smiling | And it speaks to us without saying anything | And I listen to it trembling | And I scream | I scream for you | I scream for myself | I beg you | For you | For me | And for all those who love each other | And who have loved each other | Yes I scream to it | For you | For me | And for all the others | Whom I do not know | Remain there | There where you are | There where you were in the past | Stay there | Do not move | Do not leave | We who are loved | We have forgotten you | Do not forget us | We had only you on earth | Do not let us grow cold | Always much further away | And it does not matter where | Give us a sign of life | Much later at the edge of a wood | In the forest of memory | Emerge suddenly | Hold out the hand | And save us.

3 SEVEN We're not saint nor criminals! If our love is a crime, I wish to be your victim, and if love is a sin, punish me with a kiss.

MINERVE If loving was a crime, I'd be sentenced to death.

SEVEN Let's die together tonight, because I'm not afraid to love you and to die with you.

MINERVE With me, you'll be invincible . . .

SEVEN I'm yours for life!

MINERVE For all eternity!

SEVEN I want to take you, possess you. I need you, your body, I want to cuddle and hold you tight in my arms.

MINERVE If you will love me like you love yourself, I promise to be the only true love in your life. Can you always love me with passion, often without reason?

SEVEN Yes, my beautiful . . . Yes! The passion of our love knows no boundaries; people spend their time criticising us, they ostracise us, but they could never kill this love so real and cursed. Our passion is the only light to guide us, at times a light so warm and bright, yet never too far away from us. We are, the two of us, like a song, a bird and a leaf. We wander far from the real world, into times which are not ours, but we never leave the beaten paths. The sigh we breathe is deep and heavy, yet our dreams of things to come are as light as a flake. And while we find solace in each other's arms, the wind blows to comfort us, singing a joyful song. This love is all we have, we ask for nothing but faith, where faith has left a void to fill with trust and strength. Our conscience is free, happy, and pure. Pp. 106—7.

4   The amorous conversation is over. P. 107.

15 A World Apart
1   What a torture! P. 114.

17 Le Rayon Vert (part 1)
1   Harpy, in Greco-Roman mythology, is a creature that is part woman and part bird, p. 128.

2   'Damn the rain! It's pouring: it sucks!' P. 129.

3   'What about you, little dog?' P. 129.

4   Three thunder gods. Ninhar, Sumerian deity represented in the form of a roaring bull. Lei Kung, Chinese Taoist deity carrying a drum and mallet and a chisel. Thor, Norse god, son of Odin and the earth goddess Jord, p. 129.

5   'You saved my life, little dog. Thank you!' P. 129.

6   'What's your name, little dog?' P. 129.

7   'And you? What are you doing here?' P. 130.

8   'Thank you . . .' P. 130.

18 Divination
1   A person with paranormal abilities, p. 135.

19 Denial, Anger, Bargaining, Depression, Acceptance
1   In Greek mythology, a beautiful youth and the son of the Nymph Liriope and the river god Cephissus, p. 139.

2   In Greek mythology, the nymph who fell in love with Narcissus, p. 139.

3   Literally: *I don't know what.* (An indefinable quality, especially of personality.) P. 139.

4   *Mephistopheles: Grau, teurer Freund, ist alle Theorie,* | *Und grün des Lebens goldner Baum.* [Mephistopheles: My friend, all theory is grey, and green | The golden tree of life (2038—39)]—Goethe, Johann Wolfgang von, *Faust— Der Tragödie erster Teil* (1808), p. 139.

5 Goethe, Johann Wolfgang von (b. 1749—d. 1832), German writer, *Faust*, p. 139.

6   Svengali is the name of the evil hypnotist in George Du Maurier's 1894

novel *Trilby*. The word is primarily used to indicate a person who dominates and manipulates another into doing what is desired, p. 141.

7 Inalienable condition, p. 142.

20 Le Rayon Vert (part 2)

1 'You're welcome, my dear.' P. 144.

2 Proxima Centauri is a Red Dwarf star, and the nearest star to the Sun, p. 144.

3 Gare de Lyon. One of the six railway stations in Paris, France, p. 146.

4 'Good morning.' P. 146.

5 Clermont-Ferrand. A city in the Auvergne region, France, p. 146.

6 Stuffed zucchini flowers, p. 148.

7 Flambéed orange pancakes, a typical French dessert, p. 148.

8 Château Margaux (La Mothe de Margaux), a wine estate of Bordeaux wine, p. 148.

9 In Greek and Roman mythology, the Oceanids were the three thousand daughters of the Titans Oceanus and Tethys, p. 149.

10 'I must disappear.' P. 149.

11 'No, you can't disappear, Minerve!' P. 149.

12 'Remember me, my love, when you'll meet me again . . . Never forget that I love you, and most of all that we must fight until the end, we must never surrender.' P. 149.

21 The End?

1 *Vaine illusion, mon âme te déteste*, from *La vérité* (The truth), Marquis de Sade, p. 155.

2 Full stop, p. 156.

3 Rimbaud, Arthur (b.1854—d.1891), French poet and writer, p. 157.

4 Benzodiazepines (BZDs) are a class of drugs frequently used for their sedative effects, p. 158.

5 A benzodiazepine antagonist. Used as an antidote in the treatment of benzodiazepine overdoses, p. 158.